Number 7 Spring/Summer 2003

Guest Editors: Douglas Cowie & Aleksandar Hemon
Managing Editor: Katri Skala
Design & Production: Julian p Jackson
Press, Publicity & Events: Sarah Gooderson
Marketing & Subscriptions: Emma Forsberg
Editorial Assistant: Claire Merrick

Pretext Editorial Board: Jon Cook (Chair), Julia Bell, Christopher Bigsby, Peter Bush, Patricia Duncker, Richard Holmes, Paul Magrs, Michèle Roberts, Vic Sage, Val Striker, Val Taylor.

Thanks to the following for making this magazine possible: Arts Council England, the Regional Arts Lottery Programme, the School of English and American Studies at the University of East Anglia.

SUBMISSIONS: *Pretext* is published twice a year, in May and in November. Deadline for May issue is the end of January, deadline for the November issue is the end of July. We do not acknowledge submissions and, due to the volume of material, it may take up to five months to hear back from us. If you wish to have your work returned, please enclose an SAE. For more detailed submission guidelines please turn to pages 166-167.

TO SUBSCRIBE: call 01603 592783 or e-mail info@penandinc.co.uk. One year subscription for individuals (two issues) costs £14 (UK), £16.50 (rest of world), for institutions £18 (UK), £22 (rest of world). Or visit our website <http://www.penandinc.co.uk>

Introduction: © Douglas Cowie & Aleksandar Hemon, 2003
Selection: © The Editors, 2003
Contents: © The Individual Authors, 2003
Cover design: © Emma Forsberg
Cover photo: © Simon Grange

All rights reserved. No part of this publication may be reproduced or transmitted, in any form or by any means, electronic or mechanical, including photocopying, recording or any information storage or retrieval system without prior permission.

Pretext is published by Pen & Inc Press, School of English and American Studies, University of East Anglia, Norwich, NR4 7TJ, and distributed by Central Books, 99 Wallace Rd, London, E9 5LN.

Pretext/Pen & Inc Press is a member of Inpress ltd. – Independent Presses Representation.

ISBN: 1-902913-17-5

Printed and bound by Biddles Ltd, Woodbridge Park, Guildford.

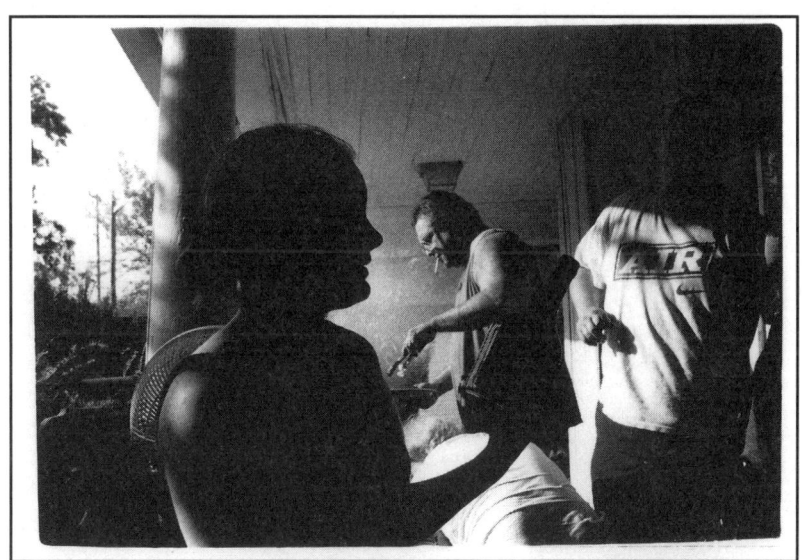

Contents

Introduction
***Douglas Cowie
& Aleksandar Hemon***   vii

Photography on pages:
iii, 30, 80, 110 & 120
Jono Tosch

Dimitroff
Rachel Seiffert   1

The Permanent Exile
of W.G. Sebald
Jens Mühling   15

Snow is all that's left
The Cherubs are Envious
To Metka
***
Tomaž Šalamun   27

Then
Claire Messud   31

Annunciation
Michèle Roberts   43

On Writers & History
***Aleksandar Hemon
& Colum McCann***   59

An Émigré Writer
on the Dragon Bridge
To Chosen Friends
A Letter Home
Aleš Debeljak   77

This Door is Not an Exit
Semezdin Mehmedinović   81

Mokattam
Ben Faccini   93

Hah!
Stef Pixner   101

The Late Flight
of Georges Braque
George Szirtes   111

The Condemned
Thomas Brussig   121

When Gravity Snaps
Owen Marshall   133

Other Creatures
Besides Ourselves . . .
Laura (Riding) Jackson   147

My Smokestack
Douglas Cowie   153

Biographical notes   161

Douglas Cowie & Aleksandar Hemon
Introduction

When I was asked to edit this volume of *Pretext*, the person who immediately came to mind to ask to work as a co-editor was Aleksandar Hemon. I'd recently finished reading *The Question of Bruno* and was recommending it to everyone who'd listen. So I wrote to him. His response, and the work we've done since, points in a curious way to the reason, I think, for writing and reading literature. When Sasha wrote back, he said that he had been reviewing W.G. Sebald's *Austerlitz*, and doing some research on the author; Max, whose impact on the life of UEA and the literary world needs no mention, had just died. *The Question of Bruno* appealed to me not only because the language seemed fresh and living, with a sense that the author actually cared about and enjoyed these words and phrases, and not only because the stories themselves felt important; I also liked it for a fairly mundane reason: because it came from a writer living in Chicago, my hometown. One of Sasha's characters, Jozef Pronek, lived and worked in a city that I knew, but which he made both familiar and unfamiliar at once. The book, and Pronek's story in particular, became a way for me, an ocean and half a continent away from home, to look again at a place I knew, to look again at my position in that place, and also to look at places and experiences about which I knew nothing.

Literature, at its best, opens a new way of seeing, both for the writer and the reader, and, perhaps more importantly, it opens a channel through which we can share, as human beings in our various places, with our various fears and problems and experiences, what it is that matters about those fears and

Introduction

problems and experiences. Literature is the road that connects someone from Sarajevo, living in Chicago, to someone from Chicago, living in Norwich, through the peculiar junction of a German with a fondness for Russian pickles.

Douglas Cowie, Norwich 2003

I am writing this while the invasion of Iraq is at full swing. My wife wept this morning reading the news about the Iraqi family that had been murdered by liberating American troops at a checkpoint, after they failed to stop. They had come across an American leaflet with a drawing of a family sitting at a table, eating and smiling, and thought that meant freedom was nearby. The family of seventeen packed into a 1974 Land Rover and drove from their village near Najaf toward the American troops. The grandfather wore his best pinstriped suit. They were waved through one checkpoint, but at the next one American soldiers, thinking it might be a suicide bomber, opened fire. Eleven members of the family died, among them seven children. An Army report declared the incident a 'mistake,' an instance of 'miscommunication with civilians.' By the time you read this, the memory of the family will have disappeared in the sea of triumphant news about the liberation of the Iraqi people. Their name was Hassan. Lamea Hassan was the name of the mother of two children who saw the top of their heads come off. The children's names were not reported.

In America today, both Orwell's nightmare and Goebbels' dream are coming true. The invasion of Iraq is called Operation Iraqi Freedom. The Pentagon refuses to discuss or provide information on Iraqi civilian casualties, and *The New York Times* omits Iraqi civilian losses from its daily body count on page two. The imbalance between the American invaders and the Iraqi Army is referred to as Asymmetric Warfare. The American invaders are just a part of the Coalition of the Willing, a non-existent entity. The journalists reporting on the invasion are *embedded* with the troops, having agreed on a number of censorship rules. The weapons of mass destruction – the alleged

Douglas Cowie & Aleksandar Hemon

reason for Operation Iraqi Freedom – have not been found by the invading troops, and Saddam Hussein is for some reason not using them, even though he's fighting for dear life. One possible reason is that they don't really exist.

The reality of war and the world defined by it is created by a coalition of the individuals willing to suspend their disbelief, to forgo their doubt, to suspend their humanity in order to support 'our' troops. From this reality the Hassans are vanished. In the great narrative of the good America, and its great ally the United Kingdom, fighting the axis of evil, their death is a glitch, an irrelevant detail, a matter of minor miscommunication.

One could reasonably ask oneself why bother with literature at a time like this. Why produce more fiction on top of the fantasy produced by Bush and Blair, not to mention all the other collective fantasies – say, the one about benevolent capitalism? How can one produce something as self-indulgent as writing when the world is being fucked up by a man who once said: 'Books are great because they often have fantastic pictures.'?

I have no answer for that. All I can say is that I hope literature can provide a place for people like the Hassans who vanish from the history written by the Bushes and the Blairs. I'm not sure that does much for Lamea Hassan, but it might do something for those who need to remember the suffering of others in the face of the lies that vanish that suffering. Literature exists for those who could easily be forgotten, for those for whom remembering is a matter of survival.

Thus *Pretext #7* was produced with the belief in literature as the opposite of miscommunication, with a clear idea that the only way to bear witness is to be embedded in the world, not with the troops. At this point, habit forces me to say: 'Enjoy the reading!' But, frankly, I wish, dear reader, that after reading this volume, you get angry and start furiously remembering all those who are about to be forgotten by history, including yourself, thus taking part in producing, along with the people in this issue of *Pretext*, what we like to call literature.

Aleksandar Hemon, Chicago 2003

Rachel Seiffert
Dimitroff

– My father is not part of my life.
Her husband says.
– The man is not a father. He is an irrelevance.
And she says.
– *If he's so irrelevant, why do you get so worked up about him?*
And her husband sighs and lies still on the sofa next to her, and she feels the breath move his chest up and down, up and down, his heart beating faster than normal.

Hannah has met her father-in-law only once, eight years ago. Before the heart problems started and the strokes. He came over for their wedding in his customary black beret and coat. His first trip abroad since the wall came down. His first time beyond the now-tattered Iron Curtain. Opposed, he announced at the reception, to what he called Jochen's American Dream, disappointed, he continued, that his son should have been so taken in.
– West Germany was bad enough, but the USA. I don't think I will ever understand.
He smiled when he said it, but nobody laughed because it was not at all clear whether he was joking.
The first stroke happened two years later and Jochen flew to Berlin. When his father was well enough, he drove him across Germany to Karl's place, Jochen's older brother. To Frankfurt am Main: temple of West German commerce. It was supposed to be a temporary solution, a period of convalescence. Six years later he is still there, and now the situation is critical.

Dimitroff

– He never lifted a finger for us, Hannah. My mother did everything.

Jochen repeats this phrase like a mantra. Most mornings, and sometimes also when they get into bed. A defensive reaction, Hannah thinks, to his father's descent into old age, his neediness. Not necessarily representative of Jochen's underlying feelings. Her own parents are both still young, not even retired yet, and she knows she cannot predict how well she will respond when their time comes. But still, Hannah is unsettled by this new, bitter side to her husband.

It is a time of many phone calls. Long distance brothers talking Brooklyn to Frankfurt. Diagnoses, updates, endless debates. Safety first or dignity, home care or nursing home, where will the money come from, what do you mean his insurance won't pay for that, so why didn't he get private cover, damn him.

– *But we have money, Jochen. Karl has money. It's not a problem.*

– Jesus Christ, Hannah. It's not about the fucking money.

Jochen swears like an American, only sounds like a German when he gets angry. Flat vowels, sharp consonants. It makes Hannah want to smile, but she is shocked too. Almost a decade together, and Hannah has never seen him so angry.

They go upstate for the weekend, get away from the phone.

– My mother left him. A couple of years later we left East Germany.

Jochen drives, and Hannah sits in the back with the twins sleeping one on either side of her, strapped in to their bright and padded seats. There are long silences, just the engine, the tyres on the road, and Hannah waits for Jochen to talk again, watching the freeway stretch off in front of them, the back of her husband's head.

– I was five. So Karl was nine or ten.

Part of Hannah is glad this is happening. Not that her father-in-law is ill, and that her husband is unhappy, but that she is hearing Jochen talk about it all. That life before she knew him, which never seemed hidden until now, when so much is being revealed.

– I'm glad she did it, you know. Took us with her.

Rachel Seiffert

Bad enough with him as a father-at-a-distance, life would have been intolerable with him as a father-close-up.

– He wasn't interested in us. What we liked doing, what we thought about things. We just didn't exist like that for him.

Jochen's harsh tones are not always easy to bear, but Hannah persists, hoping he might tell her something that will help her understand where this rawness comes from.

– *Maybe that's because you didn't live with him?*

– No. Ask Karl. He's older, remembers more. No, it was like that even before we left.

That they had no problems leaving the East is final proof for Jochen. Of his father's lack of love. He had his connections, her husband insists, he was not unimportant. Thousands of people put in applications to visit relatives in the West every year, only a fraction were granted. Pensioners were allowed to go: no longer useful, and Jochen thinks they fell into that category. The authorities were paranoid, controlling, but they were not stupid, he says. His mother's application was approved very quickly, although it was obvious to all that she would never return. Hannah stares out at the New York roadscape, listening, not questioning or interjecting, but if she is honest, she finds Jochen's logic a little difficult to follow.

– *You always say you're glad to have grown up in the West.*

– That's not the point, Hannah. He didn't care. He didn't want us.

It is this aspect that Hannah finds most implausible. After his speech at their wedding, her new father-in-law asked her to dance. Jochen had warned her that he would be difficult, had not told her that he could also be so nice. He spoke with her for a long time about her work, her family, her hopes for the future. Made it clear that he liked her, found her interesting.

– *As a person, you know. Not just as his son's wife.*

Hannah says that to her husband, watches his reaction in the rear view mirror. The sad eyes, the shrug.

What little she knows of her husband's father is that he is a communist.

– Old. Even when I was young. Fifty when I was born.

Dimitroff

1965. Hannah counts backwards to 1915 and then upwards again. 18 in 1933. She doesn't ask what happened to him under Hitler, knows only two things: that it was probably bad and that he survived.

– Oh enough now, boring, let's change the subject.
  – *Christ, J. Why do you always say that? What is that all about?*
They used to argue like this a lot, when they first started living together. Whenever they talked about Germany, which they used to do frequently because reunification was in all the newspapers and Hannah was interested and often brought it up.
  – I mean it's complicated. Not really interesting unless you're German, I guess.
  – *No. No, that's just it. The conversation will just be getting really interesting, and then you kill it with your lame 'This Is Getting Boring' excuse.*
  – It's not an excuse.
  – *Yes it is. It is. You say you can't explain it, but really you mean you don't want to. And because I'm not German and won't understand anyway, it means you don't have to. Full stop.*
And most of the time, Hannah would succeed in making her own full stop in the argument that way, and what she took to be thoughtful silence would follow. Until the evening Jochen called her bluff.
  – I don't want to talk about Nazis with you, Hannah.
He said it calmly, matter of fact.
  – We talk about Germany. We start with reunification, or with my parents, and within five minutes we're talking about Nazis. I just don't want to do it. Enough.
A direct announcement which had Hannah quickly on the defensive.
  – *But your father fought against them, didn't he? Isn't that important?*
  – And now I'm supposed to say no, so you can feel superior?
  – *You just don't want to see any good in him. You can't bear it that he did something brave and right in his life.*
  – Hannah, at the risk of sounding patronising: it is a lot more complicated than that.
Hannah was quiet, then, and Jochen was sorry to have been so

blunt. Later he did talk about it with her, briefly. Tried to explain a little of how he felt about the *Nazivergangenheit*, the Nazi Past.

– I know: it's part of my father's life, and so it is part of mine too. And of course I know it is important. But you don't know my father and you didn't grow up in Germany, West or East. You don't realize how the past sits on your shoulders there. Old Nazis, victims, the people who fought against them. Buildings, street signs, graffiti, newspaper articles.

He shrugs.

– And my father, that's all he could ever see somehow. He was blind to everything else.

Hannah remembers this conversation now, driving home from their upstate weekend. Loves her husband. Knows how difficult it must have been for him to say this, grateful that he made this effort, but still the memory upsets her. Because she knows he does talk about it sometimes. Not with her, but she has heard him on the phone to his brother and in the kitchen on Karl's last visit. In German, so Hannah couldn't understand what Jochen said, but she recognised his tones of anger, shock, sadness. Stood quietly in the hallway listening: excluded.

– Your husband is from Germany, isn't he?

The midwife's first question after the twins were born. Under her breath, conspiratorial, and with an understanding nod. What is it about him? Not tall, not blond, hardly any accent to speak of, but still unshakeably, unmistakably Deutsch.

Summer goes by, the twins' third birthday, and though Jochen resists, Hannah is persistent. She would really like to meet her father-in-law again, to know more about him. Jochen is not keen on the idea of visiting his father at first, but over the weeks, he does talk more, even starts to volunteer information.

His father wrote articles and books, on the pre-war German communist movement and the post-war division. He was considered something of an authority in East German circles, was celebrated for a while in left-leaning West German ones too. Jochen remembers finding his father's name in a book at school once, in a list of prominent anti-Nazis, but still he has no pride in

Dimitroff

his father's ideals, his achievements. On the rare occasions he speaks about them, he is at best sarcastic, at worst really mean.
— Postwar Germany according to my Dad, are you ready? In the east there are the good people, the farmers and workers. In the west, on the other hand, are the capitalists and the old Nazis, who will stop at nothing in their quest to corrupt and undermine, of course. And so to keep these fascists and exploiters at bay they, regrettably, had to build a nice big wall.
— *Come on. He's an intelligent man. It won't be as simplistic as that.*
— OK, granted, I am being less than generous. But to him the Cold War was Western aggression, and everything that happened in the East was somehow a defensive reaction. This is what I hate, you see, this hypocrisy.
— *The state was hypocritical or your father?*
— Listen Hannah: my father fought one repressive regime and then used his credentials to defend another. He was so righteous about the journalists who worked for the Nazis, and then he spent his own career writing lies and excuses.

His books are no longer in print but Hannah does find one of her father-in-law's articles in the microfiche room at the university library. The rhetoric is indeed off-putting, but the photo of the author fascinating, tight mouthed, guarded. An expression she recognises from her husband's face.

Their discussions that autumn are often tense, but they argue less and less, and sometimes when Jochen phones his brother, Hannah notices that he will also talk briefly with his father. And then, just before Christmas, a further health-scare helps Hannah win him over, her Jochen. When New Year arrives, they fly with their sons to Germany, because Jochen agrees that it is right for them to see their grandfather. That he should see his grandchildren at least once before he dies. He sends them a letter, the old man, in response to the announcement of their visit. Brief, curt, and in English: Hannah uses it as a pagemarker in the book she takes on the plane to read to the twins.

Since you are coming all this way, it would seem a waste of time to just stay in Frankfurt. I would strongly suggest that we pay a visit to Berlin.

– Out of the question.
Jochen nods at the letter over his complimentary drink.
– *Why?*
– Karl says he's not well enough.
– *Did he ask your Dad?*
Jochen shrugs. They lose altitude slowly as they approach Frankfurt and the twins rub their ears and pull their faces into exaggerated yawns.
– *He wants to go. I want to go. You and the boys can stay with your brother. I'll take your Dad to Berlin.*
– It's a bad idea, Hannah. He's too old, ill. It will be a nightmare.
– *How do you know?*
Karl picks them up at the airport. Hannah tells him about the letter and he sighs, pushing the luggage trolley ahead of him.
– He's up to something.
Hannah sits in the back again, between her sons, who are restless after the long flight. She tries to find rusks and toys in her bag and still keep an eye on her husband and brother-in-law in the front. Strains to understand what they are saying, becomes aware that she is the only woman in the car, surrounded by two generations of her male relatives: all tired and tense, with their shoulders hunched around their ears.

Her eldest male relative responds to her idea of a hire car and a road trip to Berlin with gruff enthusiasm.
– Very good, yes. I am going to bed now and shall see you in the morning.
The twins sleep in travel cots in the living room and Karl, Hannah and Jochen eat together in the small kitchen.
– At least no one will print his stuff now. Even if he could still write.
Karl rolls a cigarette, exchanges a glance with Jochen, and then tells Hannah.
– That was the worst time. After reunification, after the Stasi files were opened.
– *He worked for the Stasi?*
– Yes he worked for the Stasi, one of their informers. Informal

Dimitroff

co-workers.
– *But he wasn't the only one. Thousands of people did that, didn't they?*
– Yes, of course, but does that mean he is not responsible for his actions?

Karl doesn't raise his voice, but his tone has changed. He looks at Jochen.

– He was against the Nazis, he had suffered for the cause. I think he felt that this absolved him.

Jochen opens another bottle and nods at what his brother says. Hannah sighs at the rhetoric, thinks the sons can be just as dogmatic as their father.

– One of our cousins, Sascha, he wrote some critical essays when he was a student. Critical of the government, and so he was thrown out of university.

– *What did he write?*

– Oh, unkind things about Honecker: nothing earth-shattering. But they had been following Sascha for some time, the Stasi. And then without a degree, you see, his career chances were ruined.

– *And that is your father's fault?*

– Well it's not certain, of course, but our father lived with them for a while, in Sascha's last years of school. You never know what piece of information brought him to their attention, do you? Sascha says he read things in his file that only our father would have known.

Hannah can feel Jochen looking at her. She keeps her eyes focused just beyond Karl's shoulder.

– Do you know what he thinks now?

– No, he won't engage with me. That's what pisses me off the most. You just draw this blank with him there. No conversation, just this silence, this massive disappointment. Like we've all been a disappointment to him, the whole world, and we owed it to him to be what he expected of us, because he wanted it so much.

– *He's an old man. He was old by the time the wall came down. Maybe it's not fair to expect too much of him?*

– Oh, come on!

Jochen has been listening quietly, but he is irritated now. He raises his hands in a defeated gesture. Hannah thinks he is about

to declare the conversation boring and therefore over.
  – *Well? You don't like talking about the past with me, do you? Maybe your father is not so different?*
  Jochen blinks at her.
  – There is a difference, Hannah.
  – *Oh, really?*
  – Yes, really. He still believes the old lies.

Hannah is unsettled by the Stasi revelations. Awake on the sofa bed next to Jochen, heart pounding. She takes deep breaths, but cannot fill her lungs, regrets the late night coffee, the evening's red wine. Jochen sleeps on and she is angry. Wonders why he and Karl decided to tell her now – to change her mind about the Berlin visit? She goes over their conversation again, those glances exchanged between the brothers, the tight smiles that appeared at her questions. Hannah lies there and resents them. The way they always insist on complication, the impossibility of explanation, thinks they enjoy their Germanness and all its secrets, and after that she feels lonely and unkind.
  She wakes early, finds her father-in-law already in the kitchen. He smiles and waves a silent good morning. Hannah catches herself watching him as he pours her some tea. Can't help herself: she is intrigued. By this blunt man who can be so gentle, by this horribly compromised idealist. It occurs to her, making toast for them both, that she has only tried talking with the sons, never with the father. In her bag she has a road map of Germany, and one of Berlin. Awake now, despite her bad night, Hannah is determined to take him.

The motorway is dull and the day chilly and grey, but her father-in-law makes good driving company. He finds a radio station without commercials, tells her the names of the rivers they pass over, breaks a chocolate bar into neat pieces, lays them within easy reach on the dashboard for her.
  – Strength for the road ahead.
  Countless topics considered, discarded, Hannah talks non-stop about the twins for the first hour or so, and although their grandfather is interested, she is uncomfortable, sure he is aware

Dimitroff

that this is conversational safe ground. They come to a service station, and he suggests a coffee. He finds them a table by the window, and they smile together about the surly waiter and the plastic plants on the windowsill. Hannah remembers how they danced together at the wedding reception, tells herself to relax in the restroom mirror. Back in the car, she lets him ask her questions: is astonished by what he remembers, details even she had forgotten. That she had broken off her doctoral studies shortly before the wedding: the impossibility of combining work and research, the frustrations with her supervisor. He is sympathetic with her anger now over the cost of childcare, over having to stay at home because she cannot earn enough to pay for it.

– Yes. It was much easier in the GDR for women to work than now. Good nurseries and the state paid for them.

He smiles in the pause this produces.

– Sorry. Not propaganda. It's just one thing we did right, I think. Or at least better.

Coming into Berlin Hannah notices the weather is changing. The outside temperature reads two below zero and the clouds hang low and heavy over the city. She thinks it might snow and worries about the old man getting cold, fiddles with the dials on the dashboard until the heating system kicks in. The motorway ends abruptly and they sit at traffic lights, blinking in the dry gusts of warm air from the windscreen. Hannah's feet feel cramped and hot in her winter shoes. She can smell her father-in-law now, too. Wonders how often the home help comes to wash him. Too busy inside his own head to remember: shuffling from one room to another, leaving behind a trail of half-read books and papers.

Inside the city the traffic is stop-start and Hannah struggles with the gear-shift and the lane-changes. Her father-in-law never learnt to drive, he says, navigates badly.

The old man sits up straighter after a while, tells her they have passed into the eastern side of the city. The difference seems very subtle to Hannah: same ugly apartment buildings, same oppressive crush of traffic lanes. There are trams to add to her unease here, and they are stuck behind one for a while, the tyres singing strangely on the tracks below them.

Visibly excited, her father-in-law navigates them along one edge of Alexanderplatz before roadworks divert them up Karl Marx Allee. Smiling, shifting in his seat, the old man asks Hannah repeatedly whether she can see the TV tower in her rear view mirror.

– Look. It's an impressive sight, really.

He fidgets, turning to look out the rear windscreen, stiff shoulders straining against the belt.

– They built it to stand right in the sight-lines of the avenue. Yes, the angle should be right. Just about. NOW. *Now, Mädel*. What's wrong with you?

He stares at her.

– *Sorry. The hire car. I'm not used to it, think I should concentrate on the road.*

He coughs, turns back to look through the front windscreen at the wide, straight avenue, its imposing buildings.

– This was called Stalin Allee once. Karl Marx is much better.

He nods. Hannah can see the emphatic movement out of the corner of her eye.

– Uncle Joe. So the Americans called him, yes? American communists. Who, I understand, were banned from working for some time, put in prison.

The old man is looking at her now.

– *Yes.*

– Is that remembered in America?

Hannah changes down a gear, then up again.

– *Yes, I think it is. I believe so.*

– Did you learn this at school?

– *No. My father told me.*

She glances at him. He is listening, watching for her reaction.

– And so your father will tell your boys? Or you will?

The lights are red, she has to stop. Has no excuse not to look at him.

– *Yes, I think I will tell them. When they are old enough.*

– And now you are thinking McCarthy was nothing compared to what we did here. Yes? And I don't talk to my sons about it, do I?

He is right, or near enough, but Hannah doesn't respond. The

Dimitroff

lights change and she drives on, disconcerted by her instinct to defend, to find relative levels of wrong.
– *Is the hotel far now, do you think?*
– I have been taking us on a scenic route. Sorry. I may not see this city again.
– *OK. Yes.*
The blue signs of the underground stations go by. And then the old man directs them the wrong way up a one-way street, so Hannah has to take a few quick right and left turns to get them away from the angry drivers and pedestrians. She starts to sweat.
– Sorry. I have an old map. They changed the traffic rules along with everything else, it would seem.
Detached. Dry. Hannah unzips her coat at the next junction, catches sight of the damp patches under her arms. Feels the sweat trickle down her sides and drives and drives and says nothing even though she has a feeling they have been lost for a while because her father-in-law spends too much time looking out of the window and not enough time looking at the map.

– Here.
They are at a busy crossroads. Four lanes of traffic, trams, bicycles, an elevated train line, but he makes her pull over.
– Stop, stop. Don't go so far from the corner.
– *Is this allowed? I don't think I can park here.*
– I won't be long.
She has not pulled up yet and he is already opening the door.
– *Wait.*
But he doesn't listen. By the time Hannah has straightened up and found the hazard lights, her father-in-law is already striding back down the road to the corner. When she gets to him, he has positioned himself underneath the street-sign, and is addressing the people waiting at the pedestrian crossing in a surprisingly loud voice. Most of them cross when the lights change, but a few stay to listen.

Hannah steps forward and takes his arm, but he shakes her off, opens his briefcase and takes out a long piece of white card, on which is written, in black lettering, *Dimitroff Straße*. Home-made, the pen lines are a little shaky, but the whole thing is quite lovingly made; small brass hooks taped to the back, he holds the sign up so the gathering people can read it.

The afternoon is cold, getting dark already. A small crowd has formed around them now, fifteen or twenty people, and Hannah finds herself absorbed among them. Watching her father-in-law gesturing and shouting: a thin man in a thin coat, strangely fragile. The people around her are talking, some of the voices sharp, but others are light, laughing. A train clatters above on the elevated track, drowning the old man's voice out, he points to the street sign above him. *Danziger Straße*. It has started to snow.

Danzig she knows. *Gdansk*. Once in Germany, now Poland. But *Dimitroff*?

A young man has stepped forward out of the crowd. Blue hair and torn trousers, he makes an unlikely partner for Hannah's father-in-law, but they shake hands warmly, and then the young man takes the cardboard strip between his teeth and shins up the sign-post. When he hangs the hand-drawn words over the street-sign, a few people in the crowd cheer, one or two shout angry words, still others walk away. The blue-haired boy smiles triumphant, embarrassed. He slides down a little, hesitates, unsure whether to jump and Hannah steps forward to help him.

Six or seven people are left now, out of the original crowd, and the old man stands in the middle of them all with his watery eyes, animated hands, pink in his cheeks from the wind. Hannah wonders whether she should go and claim her father-in-law, but the conversation is intense, involved, and she doesn't know if she can stop it. She offers the boy with the blue hair a handkerchief, asks if he speaks English.

– Dimitroff was a communist, in the Nazi times. Thank-you.

He wipes his hands on his saggy trousers first, then on Hannah's handkerchief, smiles.

– This is what it was called before, Dimitroff Straße, when this was East Berlin.

The snow is settling now, blotting the letters of Dimitroff's name, turning to hissing slush under the passing cars. Voices raised and arms, the small group is oblivious to the dark and weather, debating a history of which Hannah has only the vaguest knowledge. She zips up her coat again and the young man

Dimitroff

gestures to her father-in-law.
– He is little crazy, maybe, but harmless.
– *What are they arguing about? Can you hear them?*
– Don't ask me, they're all Ossies.
– *You are not from the East?*
He shrugs.
– No, I am a student here. From Hamburg. Hey!

Hannah does not see the woman hit her father-in-law. Only the way he holds his hands over his face, beret lying on the wet pavement next to him.
– *Hey!*
Hannah puts herself in front of the old man, finds herself looking into shocked and furious faces. A second or two later, they are already disappearing, backing off, the woman who slapped her father-in-law moving away last. She is crying.

The old man sits in the passenger seat next to her, breathing and Hannah tries to drive, but her feet shake on the pedals and her arms feel useless. She turns off the main road, parks on a side street, tries to gather her thoughts, the map, the Biro circle that marks the hotel. The boy with the blue hair said it wasn't far, easy from here. She will just stop for a moment, just to calm down a little. The old man sits quietly, blinking, his shoulders curled around him. Hannah rests a hand on his back but he doesn't respond, and after a few minutes she decides to take it away again.

Trams pass, people, the street lights are on, shop signs: evening. Hannah wonders how she will describe the scene to Jochen. She feels excluded, but also in a way relieved. Not German.

After German reunification many streets in eastern Berlin were given their pre-GDR names again. One such street was Dimitroff Straße, which returned to being Danziger Straße in 1995. Georgi Dimitroff was a Communist and one of three men falsely accused by the Nazis of setting the Reichstag fire in 1933. He defended himself in court, humiliating the Nazi lawyers, and eventually winning his case.

Jens Mühling
The Permanent Exile of W.G. Sebald

On 14 December 2001, German novelist Winfried Georg Sebald, who had spent the greater part of his life as an emigrant in England, died in a car crash. Observers of that year's Christmas festivities in Sebald's native country couldn't help noticing that the writer's death had come, at least for the German publishing industry, as something of a Christmas gift. Every last bookstore's Christmas decoration featured Sebald's works. The literary press unequivocally named Sebald author of the year. A friend told me that his father, a middle-aged German physician, had received four, and given away three, Sebald novels as Christmas presents.

And yet, in spite of Sebald's sudden celebrity, his tragic death could by no means be called that of a celebrated German author. Even though he had stuck to his native language throughout his entire career as a writer, Sebald had always remained peculiarly absent from Germany's literary world. Spatially removed – he had been living in Norfolk for more than thirty years when he died – Sebald had led a rather secluded life, and had shown little inclination to participate in any kind of literary scene, let alone the German one.

This reluctance on the part of Sebald, the person, to promote the books of Sebald, the author, resulted in a peculiar situation. In Germany, his books were initially well reviewed, but otherwise went largely unnoticed. When translated into English, however, his works quickly became surprisingly successful, especially in the USA, where Susan Sontag went so far as to propose Sebald as a possible answer to her rhetorical question, 'Is literary greatness

The Permanent Exile of W.G. Sebald

still possible?' To the German public, Sebald's success in the English-speaking world came as a bit of a mystery, as no one could quite imagine how his peculiar German style could possibly be translated into English – the slowness of it, its longwinded sentences, its abundance of archaisms, its overall reminiscence of the nineteenth century.

Obviously the reception of Sebald's work in the English-speaking world and in Germany was fundamentally different. In the English translations, the foreignness of Sebald's style seemed natural and self-evident – after all, Sebald was an emigrant writing about emigrants. In German, where his style felt no less outlandish – as it seemed to date from a bygone era – Sebald's books created a kind of awkwardness, as readers were unsure whether to regard his way of writing as headstrong traditionalism or self-conscious anachronism. Either way, Sebald's success in the Anglo-Saxon world did not go unnoticed in Germany: in the years before his death, his novels finally started to find their way into the bookshops, and Sebald received the prestigious Heinrich Heine Award.

Was Sebald a German author? He wrote in German, but the use to which he put his native tongue was so different from any contemporary form of the language that this can hardly count as a criterion. Was Sebald an English author? 'I have lived here for thirty years,' he said shortly before his death, 'and yet I do not feel in the least at home here.' It seems as if there was no such thing as a home country for Sebald anymore, only, as for the emigrants in his novels, the loss of home countries. It seems as if Sebald had emigrated, permanently, into his books. Thus it would be wrong to interpret the above quote in the sense that Sebald did not enjoy living in Norfolk. He had been a teacher at the University of East Anglia for many years, was Founding Director of the British Centre for Literary Translation, and among his students and colleagues, Max – as Sebald called himself in England – is remembered with warmth.

His role as a teacher of Creative Writing classes, it may be added, was another factor which estranged Sebald from Germany's literary world, as such workshops are a phenomenon largely unheard of and often frowned upon in Germany. It was

Jens Mühling

chiefly with this background that I interviewed Sebald in 2000, about his experiences with teaching aspiring authors, and about his view of the differences between England and Germany. A conversation which might help us, now, to understand a little bit better where this permanent emigrant saw himself.

INTERVIEW WITH W. G. SEBALD

The following is a transcript of an interview with W.G. Sebald which took place in the writer's UEA office in April 2000. Sebald had agreed to pick me up at the campus cafeteria, as I did not know where his office was located. As we made our way across the campus, Sebald dropped a facetious remark about the astonishing number of people who roamed the corridors in what seemed like theatrical poses of soliloquy – it took me a moment to realize that he referred to students who were talking into their mobile phones. This seemed to confirm certain rumours I had heard on campus, according to which Sebald was not exactly the most ardent admirer of technological innovation. Thus on entering his office, the absence of a computer came as no big surprise. However, it took me more than a little courage to ask Sebald whether he minded if I taped our conversation – he didn't, and his smile seemed to humour my scruples.

Our conversation started – for no particular reason – with an anecdote about a jar of pickled gherkins that was standing on the novelist's desk. He told me it was a special, Russian, variety of pickles, which had been sent from France by a friend of his. Intended as a birthday present, it had arrived with considerable delay, which led Sebald to assume that the peculiar weight and size of the parcel must have caused the British customs authorities to suspect that it was a bomb. He insisted that I try one, noting that vinegar was 'good for all kinds of things.' In my otherwise perfectly factual notes I later found the cryptic entry 'weird comb. of sweet & sour.'

Our conversation then turned to Sebald's role as a teacher of Creative Writing students. Sebald emphasized that he saw one of his most important tasks as a teacher in warning aspiring authors about the specific difficulties encountered by professional writers.

The Permanent Exile of W.G. Sebald

Being a writer is by no means an easy profession. It is full of difficulties, full of obstacles. For a start, there is the psychology of the author, which is not a simple one. There are those situations when suddenly nothing seems to work anymore, when you feel unable to say anything. In such cases it is very helpful if someone can tell you that this happens to everybody, and show you how one might deal with such problems. In these situations it is very often the case that people neglect the research aspect. Every writer knows that sometimes the best ideas come to you while you are reading something else, say, something about Bismarck, and then suddenly, somewhere between the lines, your head starts drifting, and you arrive at the ideas you need. This research, this kind of disorderly research, so to speak, is the best way of coping with these difficulties. If you sit in front of a blank sheet of paper like a frightened rabbit, things won't change. In such situations you just have to let it be for a while.

Another important psychological problem occurs the very moment a publisher shows interest in your first manuscript. That is a most vulnerable situation for a writer. The publisher presents you with some contract, and you will sign anything, without thinking about the consequences, if only it helps to get your book published. It is very important to remind students that there are certain rules for such contracts – not many, but there are some. For example, you should never sign a contract for life, you should only sell the rights for the hardback edition, and so on. If you sign that standard contract that is used in England and Germany and anywhere else today, you will lose lots of money, which is something that few people know about. If you become a dentist, the way you earn your money is all regulated. But if you become a writer, you have to sort it all out for yourself.

On the craft of fiction

All these practical aspects of what it means to be a writer can be explained, but they cannot be conveyed in a systematic way. You cannot start the first week by explaining what working equipment is needed, how to sit down, what to read and what not to read. These issues can only be conveyed in an anecdotal way. What you also cannot do, of course, is to explain how to write a novel. The novel is much too heterogeneous a genre, all kinds of things can be a novel. There is no standard model which to take as a basis for saying: that is how a dialogue has to be structured, that is how a description has to work, this is what a characterization looks like. But there are certain basic difficulties with fiction writing, such as, for example, the tendency towards generalization, which occurs especially among people who come from an academic literary background. Whole registers of the vocabulary you acquire as a literature student are entirely useless because they are too general, because in a prose text everything has to be concrete. That is something which is not at all clear to most people.

I remember a student from my last class, who wrote something about bandstands in her text, something like 'There was this person who got interested in bandstands in London.' And that was it. So I asked her, why did she not take a look at those things, to find out where exactly they stand, how long they have been there for, what kind of people go there, what they look like, and whether there still is music being played there or not. Those are concrete forms of research, and they can be very enjoyable for a fiction writer. You cannot undertake such research if you are writing, say, a dissertation on Robert Musil. But for imaginative writing, it is indispensable to go and take a look at certain things. That seems very obvious, but like most obvious things, it is often overlooked.

On workshops

Of course it is very important to deliver criticism in an acceptable form. It does not make any sense to expose the weaknesses of a text in a polemic way. One has to be very diplomatic and ensure that the positive aspects of a text are sufficiently honoured. And then you can say: maybe you could do this part here in a different way. Imagine a text like one I recently read, which starts with the description of three photographs – 'The first picture shows this, the second picture that, and the third one this' – and this description takes up three pages. This repetitive element at the very beginning can be disadvantageous. In such a case it might be

The Permanent Exile of W.G. Sebald

better to use only one photo and make it really beautiful. That is very simple advice, and that is the kind of influence one takes. Or when somebody uses this terrible trick of accumulating adjectives, or when sentences have no rhythm. You can raise awareness to such things by talking about another person's text that is very rhythmic, but without sounding like kitsch. You can also show people that literature is, of course, about conveying emotions, but that the art is in conveying emotions without being sentimental. To give them a feeling for that border one must not cross, between drama and melodrama. All these things are demonstrable.

[When a student's text is discussed in class], the participants usually maintain a certain level of diplomacy. That has something to do with the English national psychology. I could imagine that the atmosphere would be a lot rougher in a German classroom, because Germans tend to be a lot more direct. If they don't like something, they say it very loudly, whereas the English are known for their politeness. They try not to step on each other's feet. There are these coded expressions: if someone says a text is 'interesting', then it actually means it's not very interesting. Everybody knows this, and then you either accept it or you don't. That is why this diplomacy works very well here, because people are very considerate in their social behaviour. If someone writes some horrible nonsense – which happens – then people won't go and say straight to this person's face: that's terrible what you wrote there. In Germany this kind of controversy arises very often, also in public lectures. There is always someone in the audience who has something to say, who is worried about some problem of his own, and not about the actual event. But of course you have to realize that a lot of the things that people write about are of a very private nature and that they are intricately linked with their self-respect. To undermine that would be of no use. Of course it is a problematic situation when twenty people are together in one group, because, on the one hand, everybody who entertains literary aspirations will think that they are alone with their brilliancy. On the other hand, you are faced with twenty other aspiring authors, which works against that illusion.

You also have to make it clear to people that they do not have to become writers by all means. You can also write in an amateur kind of way, there is no pressure for you to be a writer. If you really are serious about it, then it will happen at some point. But you cannot force it at a certain time, you shouldn't think, now that I have completed this course, I have to publish something by all means. It either happens or it doesn't. You have to show people that this profession has so many uncomfortable aspects that you might be better off by not pursuing it, than by condemning yourself to invent things for the rest of your life. Even if you don't become a writer after this year, you haven't necessarily wasted your time. This experience can be useful for all kinds of things. Not least it can help you to reach a higher level of self-knowledge, which is never a bad thing.

On getting a job

And I do tell people in private conversations that there are other ways of making ends meet, and that writing often doesn't work when you try to force it. People usually understand that. I also make sure to tell everybody that it is extremely important to have a profession besides writing, no matter what job it is. There are certain professions that are more suitable than others, as a parallel to this kind of work. Being a doctor, for example, won't hurt. Whereas being a dentist is not so good. You know, as a dentist you always look into the same mouths and see the same holes. You never hear anything from the patients, because they sit there like this [*pulls his mouth wide open and continues sentence in mock constrained voice*], and they cannot say anything. Whereas, as a physician, you receive valuable insight into social contexts, family stories, personal problems, that is a lot of material. Well, and the best thing probably is to be a notary. Hereditary matters. Nowhere can you see as clearly how human beings work than where money is concerned. But on the whole it doesn't really matter what you are, be it an insurance agent or a teacher or whatever – you just have to have something that will free you from the burden of having to write something every day.

Even if your first book is published by a halfway decent house, a debut novel usually won't sell more than, say, 1,500 copies. Let's

The Permanent Exile of W.G. Sebald

say it costs ten pounds, you get ten percent of that, then you've earned about 1,500 pounds. If you work on a building site for a month or two, you can easily earn the same money. Which means you will be forced to do something else anyway if you want to survive. A lot of people try to keep themselves afloat by writing book reviews, which is slave work, really. It's a lot better to be in an altogether different kind of business.

On book reviewing

Of course there is nothing wrong with book reviewing, generally, but I think it is totally wrong if writers review each other's books. That happens all the time, you know: some author reviews a contemporary writer's novel, that kind of thing, I find that idiotic. Truly idiotic. Why can't they read something else, instead of reading whatever it is that their colleagues write? Not to mention the fact that these things happen for very subjective reasons, that you make enemies, that you build up rivalry, all of which is very unpleasant. I used to write about contemporary authors, too, about Peter Handke, for example, but not after I became a writer myself. Because I simply wouldn't presume to say: that's terrible what Handke is doing these days. That's none of my business. Well, it is my business, but it is simply not my role to go and point fingers, and I wouldn't want that to happen to me either.

I hold that to be a basic rule, that you should stay away from the contemporary literary business. It has become such an industry, it is quite incredible really. I get at least two manuscripts sent to me every day, from publishers asking me to write some kind of comment for the cover. And there are all these conferences and writers' meetings and so on, one could go to three different events every week. The whole business really has become terribly inflated in recent years. The art really is in isolating yourself and letting as few things into your head as possible. To only admit those things into your head that come from a direction where no one else ever looks. That is the difficult thing.

Jens Mühling

On the literary industry

I would argue that generally it is rather bad to read books by contemporary authors. Because that is boundless – if you just think about how many thousands of novelists there are in Germany today, you will never get through with that. Due to the fact that in most countries literature is subsidized these days – just look at all these literary awards that there are in Germany today, and positions as town writers, scholarships, the German Literary Fund of the City of Leipzig, and so on. There are a lot of writers who fall into this trap very early on. They become experts at this kind of thing, they apply for this and that and thus manage to keep themselves afloat for ten or twenty years, professionalizing themselves in a ridiculous kind of way. Due to this safety net, the number of writers has multiplied by hundreds. Just look at Switzerland, there must be about five thousand published authors there today. Twenty years ago, there were only two known ones, Frisch and Dürrenmatt, and today there are two dozen just in the city of Basel. And they all meet twice a week and hug each other, while at the same time they are filled with jealousy and mutual contempt. In such an environment it is very difficult to maintain a clear view of what writing is about, because you are entangled in this peculiar rivalry. And unlike in the business world, the rivalry is very hazy, because it is disguised by these false artists' friendships. That is why it is not at all a good idea to get drawn into this world by writing book reviews, for example. The best thing is to remain outside of all of this.

On teaching creative writing at UEA

That is why it certainly makes sense if people have already acquired some professional experience [before enrolling in a writing course]. The majority of the students on this course are what you call semi-mature. They are people who have already experienced a certain amount of success and disappointment in their lives, who are not entirely naive. The last class I had was extremely heterogeneous. There were people from Hong Kong,

The Permanent Exile of W.G. Sebald

New Zealand, Canada, USA, England, Germany, people from all kinds of different backgrounds – actors, gardeners, physicians. I think that is very important, and due to the fact that so many people apply for this programme, it is possible to base your selection not only on people's texts, but also on their experiences, which sometimes can tell you a lot about whether they fit into the programme or not.

There are no specific qualifications [as a basis for judging students' entry submissions]. Originality, of course. One always hopes to read something that is shaped by the originality of an individual. There are always people who produce something which you have never read before in this form, and that is obviously the best recommendation. And then, of course, that it is not something terribly weird. That is another difference between England and Germany. That is something one knows of English literature in general, that readability recommends a text. In Germany you have all these authors who produce very bizarre and expressionistic things. They write these over-ambitious seven hundred page novels, straight out of their own head, which nobody can really follow. That is this old cultural awareness which took such peculiar turns at the beginning of the twentieth century. Expressionism still exists in Germany, and every avant-garde tendency in Germany, even today, is still infected with that old expressionism. Arno Schmidt is a classical example, definitely a very talented person, but it's all so overwrought, isn't it? There are innumerable examples of this in Germany, whereas in England, there are relatively few of them. Here, it is most people's ambition to write a readable novel.

On the differences between British and German societies

I think British society is a lot more fragmented than German society. There are all these gaps between Catholicism and Anglicanism and Protestantism and Protestant fundamentalism, between North and South and Rich and Poor and Uneducated and Forgotten and what have you. There are areas of British society which nobody really looks into, how the poor really live in certain regions, in Glasgow, for example. The more such differences there are in a society, the more interesting can you expect its literature to be.

If you are from, say, Hannover, or Oldenburg, one of these mid-sized German towns, and you had a proper high school education, come from a normal middle-class family, always have a certain amount of money in your pocket, then it is very hard to start writing with such a background. Because writing is always provoked by certain extreme experiences which a person has made. So when you have always had it relatively good, something is missing. That is often a problem among these Swiss authors, who have always had enough money, who have a heap of Frankens lying around in the bank from their fathers and grandfathers – because money has always existed in Switzerland – and who are married to a doctor who also earns a heap of money. They take care of the household and work as a writer at the same time. They pick up the kids after kindergarten, and then they sit down in the afternoon and write some extremist text about child pornography. There is something wrong with such a situation. That is very different from, say, Jean Genet writing about the extreme experiences in his life, because Genet didn't simultaneously play Lego with his children. And that is why I think experience, no matter in what form, is important, and I mean a kind of experience that is different from the mainstream. The more homogeneous a society is, the more writers it will produce, but the less good writers. That is the phenomenon we have in central Europe today.

W.G. Sebald was born in Wertach im Allgau, Germany, in 1944. He studied German language and literature in Freiburg, Switzerland, and Manchester. From 1970 he taught at the University of East Anglia in Norwich, England, becoming professor of European literature in 1987, and from 1989 to 1994 was the first director of the British Centre for Literary Translation. His three previous books, Vertigo, The Emigrants *and* The Rings of Saturn *have won a number of international awards, including the* Los Angeles Times *Book Award for fiction, the Berlin Literature Prize, and the Literatur Nord Prize. In 2001 he published his final novel,* Austerlitz, *to critical acclaim. He died in a car accident,*

The Permanent Exile of W.G. Sebald

in December 2001, aged 57. After Nature *(Random House, 2002) and* On the Natural History of Destruction: With Essays on Alfred Andersch, Jean Amery, and Peter Weiss *(Random House, 2003) were published posthumously.*

Tomaž Šalamun
Poetry

SNOW IS ALL THAT'S LEFT

I think about God instead of thinking
of snow. Not true.
God thinks about me and eats me.
No one thinks about anyone.
A little cart goes down the road.
Snow falls when it falls.
God is a perfect stranger, he is not planted by anyone.
I'd like to be planted like a willow.
I'd like to be planted like grass.
And then fall upon it like snow, softly.
We would fall asleep and uncover God's blanket, my
skin, and disappear in the street, into the night.
Yesterday I walked by the swinging doors.
Doors from knees to chest.
I wanted to go in to see if the angel was there.
There was an old man with a sombrero.
With dark skin and even darker eyes.
I spilled tequila.
I knocked it back.
The sound was not that of opening
a pipe for water to flow.
I need to drink tequila
I need to be a tree, planted in the earth, and
push the door.
I need to meet an angel.

*Translated from the Slovenian by
Peter Richards & Ana Jelnikar*

Title   *Tomaž Šalamun*

To Metka

If I set fire to the white frame of the house, will the flame burn
brighter then the weight falling off our bodies?
Brighter than the samba? Brighter than my watery head?
I'm in the snow, you are dancing. Under the gigantic

green trees with your sad watery eyes.
We're listening to the rhymes and slippers of your paintbrush.
Of meadows in which you see moss and what's under
the mixed moss. A white lynx scratching in a dark green throat.

Does the sky stop itself up and rattle? Where do you rest?
In an avalanche or on the earth? I gorge myself here, gorge
myself,
swelling to keep from being torn apart in the heights

by the clouds, pink, blue, and violet, and the flowers,
like Tiepolo, the air cleansing itself behind him,
before the light floods and crushes us.

Translated from the Slovenian by Christopher Merrill & Ana Jelnikar

***

You are my angel.
A mouth dusted with chalk.
I'm a servant of the ritual.
The untouched.

White mushrooms on a white field,
In the horizon of fire.

I am walking on the gold dust.

Translated from the Slovenian by Joshua Beckman & Tomaž Šalamun

Poetry

THE CHERUBS ARE ENVIOUS

flesh in blossom, frank o'hara
I looked at your hands, pictures of heaven
I straightened out the alarm clock, april images
I blotted local systems, built the day
he: churches fell she: dichotomy, quakers
o, o, funny, he: the king of the scene she: the name of cartoons
she is gulping oxygen, red grass, owners exist
dusty attics, a generation of steamboats
flowers in waterfalls, entering Katmandu
princesses, roads in ice
workers in a landscape where tooth rulers are
they rush, they sense, how knowledge comes through their mouths
how mothers crowd the genuine article
how the two-month-old puddle leans upon
far thrown in the dust, bare feet
rapture, the mortar in the window
with teeth and palm on brown hat, a film director
on public scale! on public scale! on the sun! on the sky!
where crickets sunbathe on posts
with carburettors cut through on the right side of the castle
in ivy, with a puma, with religious pioneers
don't use an angel face
a soap, towels, dead men
chicken noodle landscape, polish oil
smoke screens, hairy people whistle through their fillings
cultural attachés in Washington, masons
white carved glass, short zippers
oval crackers, maps with chocolate
people, planetary bulls
the seed is here, the night is here
little men climb from the trees
as salamun washes the animals, there must be light
grace of god, their upright bread.

Translated from the Slovenian by Joshua Beckman & Tomaž Šalamun

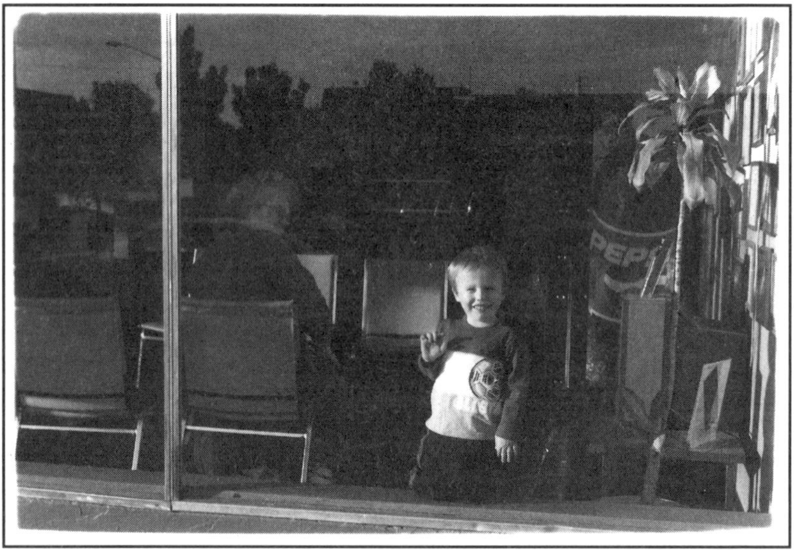

Claire Messud
Then

The Maguires' garage was immense, or seemed so, and dimly lit, in such a way that we, the children, cast strange shadows or were in shadow, and you couldn't, as a result, tell how many of us there were. Not many, in truth – fewer than a dozen – running in arcs and circles and laughing, our laughter resonating against the slick concrete floor and the bare walls so that the space was as alive with sound as with movement. At the centre of our games glimmered a car. Not a grown-up car, but a child's car, vermilion, finned, of shiny tin, with plump black tyres and space enough for only a driver at its glossy wheel, powered by pedals, by the furious pummelling of small and greedy feet. Driving the car was the afternoon's prize, squabbled over, traded, aspired to, lost. Its owners, the three freckled Maguire children in whose garage we played, were moderately magnanimous, or else their mother was, and almost every child, including my sister, took a turn speeding the rectangular track beneath the naked looming bulb.

But I, all of three, would not, could not, drive the car. I loitered, baffled, at the murky edge of our communal play, trying my damnedest to fathom the facts: this had been *our* car, my sister's and mine. That morning, when we woke, this car, our Christmas car, splendid, red, and yes, tinily dented, only we knew where, had held pride of place among our toys, in our house, at the other end of the cul de sac, over the stream. And now – it was almost suppertime, and we would all soon be called, in our twos and threes, to scatter to our various kitchens and their rituals – and now, our car was no longer ours. It was theirs.

Then

And yet it, and we, and they were all still much as we had been. I couldn't understand it.

This is one of my earliest memories, preceded only by two others, one dream-like and one precise. This moment of this afternoon I recall because of the ache, a visceral, a terrible, but I knew even then unsayable, ache at the loss of our prized possession. I didn't know how I had loved it until I knew it was no longer mine.

We were moving to Australia and had had, that morning in Stamford, Connecticut at the dawn of the 1970s, an immense tag sale, dispensing all our more cumbersome toys to the neighbourhood kids for pennies. A few treasures – the toy stove and its battery of dented pots – were stored against our future, to be opened, too late, in 1977 in Toronto, when we no longer had any use for them and disdained the very nicks and cracks that had made them truly ours. But for Australia, for life as it was to come, we could take only what would fit in our suitcases: Michka, my Russian bear, all of eight inches tall with a tiny red silk nose; white blanket, already holey and dishevelled, crocheted by my French grandmother and indispensable; and a stuffed grey felt elephant with wobbly knees who ought to have stood up but couldn't, any longer, for which we loved him more rather than less.

But our car: less than a year old, grudgingly shared between my sister and me, and haughtily loaned to our neighbours within the confines of our yard – and never, surely never, to the nasty Maguire boys, and only under duress to their snotty little sister – this car would not cross the ocean. It was sold at our sale – the very first toy to go – and that afternoon, as I pretended in the Maguires' garage that I didn't care a fig, I ached. I ached even for my sister's loss, and thought her at once treacherous and impressive for actually driving the car, zooming about as if she could enjoy it. I ached enough to remember it, always.

It would be months before we had a home again, and a car like that, never. (Similarly, in my early childhood, my Canadian grandmother had, in her garage, an aged brown Jaguar, which I recall, for some reason, as velvety, with a wood-panelled dashboard and elegant, luminous dials; and yet it, without explanation, while we were at the other end of the earth, ceased to be hers and was replaced by a sky-blue Toyota Corolla, later corroded by rust and therefore, always, in my mind's eye, corroded by rust, a small and graceless conveyance with cold black vinyl seats. And when, again, would she have a car like the Jaguar? Never. Indeed, the Corolla would be my grandmother's last car altogether, as during those years she lost her sight, by agonizing degrees, to macular degeneration, and very soon, before we even returned from Australia, was unable to drive at all.)

Before Australia, my parents had to prepare the way, and so they left us – in school, though barely – with Grandma in Toronto while they flew to Sydney – a long way, in 1970; a much longer way than it is today – and found us a place to live, and a school to attend. On account of quarantine laws, they oversaw, too, the division of our two dachshunds, uncle and nephew, Big and Small: the former would go to his native France to live with my paternal grandparents and dine on table scraps, while the latter, smaller, wilier, with more soulful eyes, would stay in Canada and become the bane of my grandmother's existence, ultimately tripping her and spraining her ankle on a winter's walk to nearby frozen Grenadier Pond (the same pond into which my mother in a much earlier winter, as a girl, had fallen, through the ice, while walking one of a succession of family spaniels all named Nicky.)

In Toronto, in my grandmother's house, my sister and I were always happy. Which is not to say that we did not bicker, as bickering, from very early on, was our mode of interaction; but that we adored my grandmother, and trusted her absolutely. She was rightly sized for us, at little over five feet, and stout, with pillowy white hair and a pillowy bosom (which we did not then know to be made of foam and removed, nightly) and an array of silky nylon dresses that seemed designed for hugging. She had small but firm arthritic hands that held ours warmly and allowed us the freedom to finger their odd bends and warts and calluses, and the smooth, distinct ridges of her fingernails. In the mornings, in a bedjacket with large buttons and her near-invisible hairnet (which we loved to pluck) upon her curls, she would invite us, one on either side of her, into her high old

Then

marriage bed to play games – 'I Spy', or 'I packed my bags to go to Boston' – and to sing songs – '. . . every little wave had its nightcap on, nightcap, white cap, nightcap on . . .'; 'Roll, those, roll those pretty eyes, eyes, that, I just idolize . . .' – seemingly for hours. And how she fed us: daily (in memory, at least), she granted us our favorite meals: Campbell's tomato bisque soup and salami sandwiches, or Chef Boyardee ravioli, eaten on the sun porch overlooking her steeply tiered back garden, my sister and I vying for the privilege of sitting on the stepping stool and so being able, with our feet, to swing its folding steps in and out, in and out, with spooky creaks, throughout the meal.

Even our grandmother's basement was a treat, its cement painted oxblood, its warm air scented by laundry soap with, in one corner, the basket into which miraculously issued the socks and pyjamas dropped through the chute two flights up. We had a tricycle down there – no match, of course, for our lost car, but still – upon which we whirled around and around the red floor, avoiding the dip in its centre that was, most mysteriously, a drain. And on the half-landing between basement and kitchen, by the side door, the house's other secret and delicious feature: the hutch for the milkman, a box opened from both inside and outside the house, in which, still, in our early youth, milk, butter, eggs and juice appeared magically before breakfast.

We were only a couple of months, at that time, in my grandmother's house, and I attended a bilingual nursery school in the yard of a church. I went by carpool, while my sister set off elsewhere, and I made, in that short time, a best friend named Renée, next to whom I sat each morning and afternoon in the car, and whom I would discover again, briefly, many years later when we moved back to the city, and would have nothing in common with. It was there, in the playground, that I first learned – oh, endless lesson! – that I was not as clever as I believed myself to be. It must have been warm, because my legs were bare; and I remember the shafts of sun around me, dappling the cement, and the shadow of the church wall rising to my left, and the hubbub of screaming children on the slide and the monkey bars. But in my memory, I am completely still, a fixed point in the maelstrom, when upon my inner right thigh

Claire Messud

settles what I take to be a fly. I remember the furry tickle of it, the movement which I took to be its mandibles rubbed; and I remember triumph with which I thought: 'I will kill this fly, fast as fast. I will slap my thighs together and he will be dead, nasty fly.' But alas, the fly was a bee.

When we got to Sydney, our new house awaited us. Although then I had nothing to compare it to, it was, and remains, the grandest place I have ever lived: 93 Wollesley Road, Point Piper, a large mottled brick house with a circular drive and a high wall around the garden, a short walk from a little beach and a short drive from our school in Vaucluse.

The house was fronted by a portico, and before it, a small fountain, in which a bronze Pan piped eternally. A walled garden lay down an alley on the kitchen side, doubtless intended for vegetables but unplanted, and in it the owners had constructed a large chicken wire aviary, left empty and forlorn. The lawn on the opposite side of the house, off the living room, broad and rolling and verdant, headed downhill towards the sea, and against its furthest edge nestled a row of fruit trees referred to, grandiosely, as 'the orchard'.

The rooms in the house were numerous and vast, the gloomy kitchen cavernous enough to echo, with two sinks and a great stretch of black and white linoleum and – or has an older child's imagination merely inserted it there, stolen from British children's books of yore? – a green baize door to mark it off from the public rooms. The back staircase led up from this kitchen to the suite my sister and I shared, a bedroom and off it a large, windowed expanse dubbed 'the nursery'. And off the landing of that back staircase, the service flat waited, two rooms and a bathroom overlooking the empty aviary, with their own locking door. The house was full of the owners' furniture, while they, knighted now, were off being grander still in London for a time. The surfaces throughout were dotted with knick-knacks – Dresden shepherdesses, heavy cut glass ashtrays – all of them valuable and all hazards to our small and eager limbs, so that we were, from the first, discouraged from playing downstairs. I liked best the little cloakroom just to the right of the front door,

Then

which was small but had ceilings just as high as those in every other room, so it felt like a tall, narrow box; and the room off the dining room, a second, less formal dining room, indeed, which reminded me of my grandmother's little sun porch, and overlooked the broad lawn. The furniture in that room was of dark green wicker and the chairs were, befittingly, like thrones, their backs a peacock's fan.

My sister and I were enrolled at one of several girls' schools in the city. Ours, Kambala Church of England School for Girls, had (and still has) a magnificent property in Rose Bay next to the Sacred Heart Convent, looking back, from its green slope, upon the glistening bay, at the opera house and the harbour bridge and the winking white sailboats dotting the water. But in our first years, we travelled on, beyond the main campus and down the hill to Vaucluse, to the elementary school, Massie House, housed in a white stucco mansion among other grand houses in their enclave by the sea.

There, at first, I wore a yellow pinafore over my clothes and spent the afternoons pretending to nap, with a dozen other reluctant nappers, in rows of folding cots in a large, darkened room. I greatly envied my older sister her complicated uniform and its religious rules, and felt tremendous pride when, at whose hand I do not know, I was sprung early from the confines of the nursery and kitted out for kindergarten.

We had uniforms for summer and for winter. The former was a grey and white checked shirt-dress, belted, worn with a straw boater banded in grey, with the school crest upon it. The latter was a grey tunic, beneath which we wore white shirts (with Peter Pan collars, while at Massie House) and grey and gold striped ties (bow ties, with the Peter Pans), and topped by a grey felt hat, again banded with the crest. Grey socks; black oxfords; grey jumpers; grey blazers (with gold piping); grey knickers; grey ribbons (compulsory, if your hair touched your collar). We had gear, too: coloured wooden rods with which to learn arithmetic, stored in grey plastic boxes with our names on them. We had colour-coded booklets, a system called SRA, by which we learned to read, and they were kept in grey file cabinets in the classroom, to be shared by all. We had gym clothes, including regulation black sandshoes, and tasselled girdles to denote our sports house (mine was red, for Wentworth). We had plastic covers for all our textbooks, lined, sometimes, with wrapping paper, in order to make them more attractive. Later, we would have sewing baskets, wicker boxes with little handles and looped clasps, in which carded embroidery threads in riotous colours grew, inevitably, fatally entangled. Our bookbags were of hard brown vinyl, square cases held in our tiny hands to thump against our legs and tagged, like luggage, with our names and addresses.

Young ladies always stood when a teacher came into the room. Young ladies walked in crocodile file, two by two, when moving from one room to another, one building to another. Young ladies did not run. There was to be no eating in uniform in public. Hats must be worn at all times in the street. Young ladies did not yell. Young ladies strove, at all times, to be a credit to their school. The rules and rituals were endless, a language to be mastered and then – but stealthily, stealthily – trifled with. You learned the rules so that you might break them when the need arose.

From the first, I loved that school, everything about it, and granted my devotion to each demure and spinsterly schoolteacher with the same fervent passion: cross-eyed Miss Watt, whose myopia and bottle-bottom glasses gave her an underwater aspect, and whose tubular calves I still see swaddled in their thick tights bunched above black orthopaedic shoes; smooth and quiet Miss Dixon, the headmistress of Massie House, universally adored, with her pale freckles and tidy golden bob; the brusque and spotty Miss Clarke, whose spiky hair was always a little greasy, and whose difficult affection I was particularly proud, by the end of the year, to have won. My sister travelled upwards, of course, always a year ahead of me, and I took her lessons – her especial fondness for Miss Dixon, for example – to heart.

When we were at Massie House and living on Wollesley Road, my mother found a driver to take us to and from school. His name was Gary, and he can barely have been twenty, but to us he was a man, with his stubbled chin and the blond fur along

Then

his arms. He drove a battered blue station wagon, and picked up more than half a dozen little girls each day. Whether this constituted his sole employment we never knew, but he was prompt and reliable in spite of his scruffiness. At first I didn't care for his car, or at least, not for the front seat: none of us did, because whoever sat next to him had to suffer his spidery hand upon her thigh, moving, often up beneath her skirt almost to her knickers. We squabbled each afternoon for the safe seats in the back (in the mornings, the front fell to the hapless two who were picked up last), until I discovered that Gary would pay me two cents a day to massage his shoulders while he drove, and that this employment not only swelled impressively the belly of my piggy bank, but also spared me, in permanence, the loathed front seat.

It wasn't for some months, until I offered to massage my father's shoulders and he registered horrified surprise at my proficiency, at my even knowing what a massage might be, that Gary's oddities came to light at our house, and our subscription to his service was abruptly stopped. (I distinctly recall, however, the dwindling number of girls in the wagon over that time: each girl, then, must have confided to her parents the horrors of the front seat, and was quietly removed from harm's way. No parents rang each other, though, or they did not, at least, ring my parents; perhaps because we were foreign, or perhaps because each outraged adult assumed the others knew. Or indeed, in keeping with the tenor of the times, because nobody wanted to make a fuss about something so trivial.)

Gary was replaced by my frazzled mother in her brown Austin mini, a more salubrious but altogether less prompt chauffeur, for whom we waited at the curb many times while torturing ourselves with the grisly possible causes for her tardiness: car crashes, conflagrations, a broken neck at the bottom of the long front stairs on Wollesley Road. Her chief advantage, when she arrived, lay in her willingness to drive us directly to the Milk Bar in Rose Bay for chocolate bars, or, better yet, to the neighbouring bakery, from which we emerged with slabs of chocolate cake, or sticky buns, or hard-frosted confections named lamingtons, which we ate openly, cheerfully,

Claire Messud

in our uniforms with our hats off, protected from the rules, from the marauding prefects who might sentence detention, by our magical parent, whose own lips bore tell-tale traces of chocolate or sugar.

During this time, swiftly, we learned the rules of the language, its codes as vital for survival as those of the school or of Gary's blue car. We learned to speak with Australian accents, broadening certain vowels and closing others, so that we would sound the same as our friends; although at home, we spoke to our parents like little Americans; and in the car, spoke one way in the back seat and another when addressing the front. We learned the slang ('Have a fab Chrissy!') and the popular songs (I'm not sure I have ever heard a recording of 'Seasons in the Sun', but I know its lyrics perfectly from the playground), and the references, learning by heart the advertising jingles off the television, which I can sing to this day ('Sun and surf, it's all so great, here in Queensland, super state!'). We let fall the North American trappings as efficiently as we had let go of our little red car, and we learned not to look back, and not to look forward, but instead to read the present, to parse its details as efficiently as possible, in order – this was surely the hope; it remains, always, the hope – to pass for a native. (I do this in spite of myself wherever I am, to this day, including, and least successfully, in France, because I am half-French; but always with an awareness that it cannot wholly succeed, that I will be found out, and with the question, in the back of my mind, of how much of a freak, how far outside the realm, I appear to the others to fall. By how far have I failed, in my local transvestism?)

To return, then, to our grandmother's that first Christmas was a shock, our first introduction into the ongoing schizophrenia of the unsettled life. From Sydney's incipient summer, its clammy heat, we flew through days and nights to the snowy lawns of western Toronto, to the hedges and porches festooned with Christmas lights and the brown slush of the streets. We found my grandmother and her house and its beloved contents the same as we had left them, though frayed somewhat by the anxious teeth of the dachshund, Small, who, missing us, or most importantly, missing Big, with whom he had

Then

shared everything since birth, had taken to gnawing the edges of the broadloom and scraping at the doors with his claws. We rediscovered our little room, and, in the mornings, our grandmother's high bed, and her hairnet, and her particular powdery, perfumed smell, as if we'd never abandoned them; and the trike waited in the basement, and the stepping stool on the sun porch, its seat patched with silver duct tape, still creaked in its satisfying rhythm.

But the Jaguar was gone, the turquoise Corolla in its place; and Joy, the girl next door who had been our playmate, had moved away to the West Coast; and most painfully for my mother, my grandmother had sold the family summer cottage without informing her, complete with all its contents, on the grounds that it was too much work to keep up, but actually in some sinisterly ruthless way to teach us all, her daughter most of all, that you cannot go away and come back to find things the same, that leaving has consequences, some of them bitter, that you cannot, indeed, ever come back at all. This, of course, was something that my father, *pied-noir* and son of a peripatetic family, child of the Second World War, had already long ago learned and would spend a lifetime imparting to his children; but it was new, then, to my mother, who wept at the loss of a place she had loved, and loved with her father in it, and he now long dead; and new, too, to my sister and to me, who were young enough to accept that this was just the way of the world, and to turn on the television and memorize another set of advertising jingles and to try, for a few weeks, in the company of cousins and of other Christmas visitors, to pretend – in our new furry hats with pom-poms, and our coats with velvet collars, of no use in Australia – that we were a legitimate part of this world, too, and not mere pretenders.

On the Sunday before Christmas, my grandmother took us all to her church downtown, the central United Cathedral which is surrounded by missions and a park in which the indigent sleep. She was a fixture in that place, as old as the century, having paraded with her congregation and walked into it as a girl when the United Church of Canada was formed, sometime in the 1910s, belonging there as much as it is possible to belong. She

Claire Messud

thought, perhaps, that the force of her connection extended to the rest of us, that because she was at home we were perforce also; and in this spirit she dispatched my sister and me, against our wills, to the Sunday school in the basement.

There, bathed in hideous fluorescence, with the murky grey of the Toronto winter sifting balefully through the small, high windows, we were perched at the front of the room by the Sunday school teacher, a buxom girl with crooked teeth and a surprising persistence in interrogation. With a circle of moon-faced, bug-eyed, pallid children around us, their gaze upon our unusually tanned skin (it was summer in Sydney, after all), their ears cocked for our antipodean syllables (perhaps we were not so adept at shifting from one English to another as we imagined?), we were introduced as two Australian visitors, there to tell the others what it was like 'down there'.

I remember to this day the scarlet fury of my cheeks, the twitching misery of that hour, to which I responded with sullenness and a furrowing of the brow, while my sister gamely chatted and revealed snippets of our private, our secret other life, as if it were less real, or of the same reality, as the dingy brick and grey linoleum and folding chairs around us, of the same reality as the brittle, bosomy instructor or the indistinguishable Christian children who were her charges. Like riding the red car: my sister just got on with it, which, in time, I would learn from her, to smile and smile and be a villain, and that our hold on this other life, like our memory of the red car, was not the less for that.

Because the truth is that the other life, the hidden one, or ones, is not the less real, nor as real, as the life before us. It is infinitely more real, blooming and billowing in the imagination in its fecundity and fullness, coloured and enlivened by so many objects, so many sounds and smells, so many minute moments that can never, never be imparted. It is wrong to think of them as past: Sydney, then, was just beginning; and Toronto was, in our lives, a constant, and then, for a time, a home; just as Toulon, my father's family's chosen place, remains my life's one unbroken link to this day. They were concurrent presents, and presences, and somehow because of this, and magically, they have remained always present.

Then

If I crossed the ocean today, would I not find my childhood friends dangling from the monkey bars, their ties flailing and their crested hats in a pile upon the grass? Would I not find my grandmother, at the end of another long journey, with Small upon her lap and her warped fingers reaching out to hold mine? And somewhere, even, if I could only travel that distance – a few short hours as the crow flies, but unimaginably far in truth – is the red car with its glimmering fins, and the house by the stream, the first bed and the first home, known to me only as a place where always, already, I didn't quite belong.

Michèle Roberts
Annunciation

Marie was ready for the angel when he whirred into her life: used to strange men, desperate for her to notice them, accosting her; burly toddlers whose catcalls beat like fists on her shell. She'd swallow anything, Marie, her classmates scoffed. Oyster girl: open-mouthed and vulnerable and soft. That was a common definition of a young woman in the 1960s, and that's how the nuns in the grey stone convent tried to bring them up. Marie was a success at school: pure; that's to say ignorant; and therefore defenceless. Easy prey. Ever so nice and willing and eager to please and no idea of standing up to anyone in authority. Raised to obey, to defer to her olders and betters; never to say no to anyone who told her what to do; not to say boo to a goose.

Slag or saint – you were allowed to choose. Bad girls, basically common, chewed gum on the street and strutted home hatless, gossiped about periods and pubic hair and French kissing, despised grammar, were not allowed to learn Latin, accepted their utter worthlessness. In the sixth form Marie was appointed Head Girl. She had to cruise the cloakrooms at lunchbreak and report miscreants applying make-up. The bad girls waved their mascara wands at her; smirked at her shiny nose and curly hair.

Marie left school at eighteen. She considered becoming a nun but decided to get a taste of the world first, in order all the more grandly to renounce it later on. She started work as a clerk for the GPO. Her job was in the addressograph office. Less of an office; more of a production line. The two older women she worked with, Floss and Margaret, were kind, always ready to give a hand when Marie got stuck or made a mistake, but she didn't know

Annunciation

how to respond to the raucous banter they shouted above the noise of the heavy machines. In those pre-computer days you punched letters and numbers onto metal printing plates. You could hammer the type and smoke at the same time. Floss and Margaret had the radio going all day long, and a counterpoint flow of endlessly inventive teasing. They batted saucy jokes back and forth, roaring when Marie didn't get them.

To celebrate her freedom and her first pay packet Marie threw away the brown tweed skirt and yellow cardigan she'd worn at weekends for the last four years; she bought a scarlet coat, a bright blue tartan shift dress, some white lace stockings and a black suspender belt, and a pair of white high-heeled boots. She bought eyebrow tweezers, curlers, hair spray, a ladies' razor, pale beige foundation, pale pink lipstick, pale blue eyeshadow.

She didn't know how to make friends. Non-Catholics had been frowned upon at home. She told herself she enjoyed feeling independent. Her workmates shrugged when she avoided the canteen at lunchtime and ate her cottage cheese sandwiches by herself. At night she went out on her own. She discovered she didn't like going to the cinema, though, because the minute the lights dimmed men would arrive in the neighbouring seat and start to bother her, nudging and whispering. Sometimes they opened their flies and fingered their thing and she'd have to get up and leave and miss the film. She didn't complain to the manager. It was just how men were and you put up with it. The girls at work, when she mentioned it during a coffeebreak, said she should take it as a compliment: I should be so lucky! One day Floss read out a report of a rape in the newspaper: ooh I can't wait! They fell about laughing.

Marie was certain that if she met a good man she would recognise him immediately, because he'd treat her so well. She was willing to put up with being lonely while she waited, but in the interim she met a lot of weirdos. When you walked around the city men sprang out at you from every crack and every crevice, edging much too close, not even bothering to chat you up, just murmuring obscenities, rubbing up against you, asking how much you charged. It was because she was young, and on her own. She had that wide-eyed look of the newcomer to the city and they were just trying their luck.

Michèle Roberts

Other punters were more subtle, stepping up to her breezily as though they'd already met, smiling, asking the way somewhere, asking the time. Before she knew any better she let several of these men steer her into a pub, buy her a drink then take her back to their hotels. She thought they wanted a chat and felt rather daring going up to their rooms. She let them fuck her. It was what she was there for, wasn't it: they'd bought her a gin and tonic, which showed she was willing. She didn't know you could say no. She'd been brought up by the nuns to be accommodating and polite. So you couldn't call it rape. She lay there and went through the motions and felt nothing. It's odd having sex with people you don't fancy, them lying over you slathering and groaning and jerking while you're not even liking their smell or the look of their prick. Marie didn't like pricks much at all: mottled flobby things men'd push into her hands and make her caress. She didn't like the slime of their come on her belly either, cold like congealed eggwhite. But it was all one in the eye for Mum and Dad and the parish priest and the nuns. Little whore they'd have called her if they'd known. But Marie never went home again and so they didn't find out.

The psychiatrist she had to see later on said: you pretended to be so innocent but you wanted it, didn't you? Why deny what you did? Why can't you take some responsibility for what happened? Marie tried to explain that Catholics believed in obedient girls. You did what you were told. That was what religion meant. But the psychiatrist didn't believe her: you seek out situations of seduction. Marie wondered: so that was what it was called.

After a while she learned to keep her eyes down in the street, and not to look around her; so fewer men bothered her. Having given up on cinema she went to evening classes instead: art history, watercolour painting, French, and dressmaking, subjects that didn't attract the kind of men who were always trying to get her into bed. Then she'd come home, quite cheerful, to her bedsit in Earl's Court.

At the time of meeting Joe she'd just begun sharing a flat in Museum Street with three of the girls from work. An old mansion block. Kitchenette, lounge, four beds in one room, bathroom on the floor below. You couldn't bring a boyfriend back to spend the

Annunciation

night because there was no privacy, so her three flatmates decided to hold an orgy instead.

Marie had been there a month. She stayed and watched the sexy proceedings for a while because she didn't know what else to do or where else to go. She felt safer indoors than braving the streets on her own. She knocked back a few halves of cider, and then it was easy just to flop on a brown velvet floor cushion and pretend nothing strange was happening.

Four men, fellow clerks from work, arrived. People she knew to say hello to. They helped roll back the mustard nylon carpet and push the furniture out of the way. They took the nubbly armchairs and formica coffee table into the bedroom, upended the crimson velvet settee, and put down beanbags for sitting on. Marie assumed it was going to be a normal Saturday night party. She got invited to parties sometimes. Sooner or later the lights would flick off and there'd be groping in the dark and yelping. This lot were all laughing and chatting and joshing each other just like they did at work. They carried in a case of beer and poured peanuts into saucers and arranged ashtrays.

Her flatmates suspended black sheets from the walls, laid a black sheet on the floor, and lit the room with black candles. They inverted a crucifix and propped it up over the fireplace, placed a plastic skull, such as you'd buy in head shops, on the mantelpiece, and pinned up a tatty poster of a goat. Though Marie had been brought up such a good Catholic she didn't feel at all outraged. She just felt she was in a cold ashy place. It was like sitting in an empty grate. She realized she didn't believe in God any more. There was no God to be offended by what this lot were getting up to. They needed to feel daring and wicked in order to have group sex. The satanic decorations were a way of spicing things up.

At first the atmosphere was simply boring, like the beginning of parties often was, before everyone got drunk. Her flatmates burned joss sticks and played rock music and passed joints around and slung down the beer. Marie sat by the record player trying to be invisible.

Eventually everyone started dancing and taking their clothes off at the same time. All those white bums and white penises joggling around. Such soft bodies. It wasn't the nakedness Marie minded, so much as having to see everyone at work the next day fully dressed, knowing what they'd looked like the night before waving their bits about, yet pretending she didn't. Suits and dresses and cardigans are supposed to cover you up but they don't, not if someone's seen what you look like underneath. She didn't see why she should be forced to look at so many naked people all at once. One at a time was bad enough.

She riffled desperately through the record collection and put on some Bob Dylan and pretended to read the record sleeve. There was a bit of mucking about with the crucifix, the men stroking each other with it, taking turns sliding it into the girls' fannies. When her three flatmates sorted themselves out a partner each, and lay down on the floor, and began having sex, Marie felt a bit in the way. Also she realized that the fourth man was making his way across the room towards her.

She was sitting there, wasn't she? That's what the psychiatrist pointed out. So she'd joined in. Sort of. She didn't know how to leave. She lived there, after all. Where could she go? The bedroom was full of the sitting-room furniture and the kitchenette had no door. He must have thought she was saying yes. She felt stuck, as though she were drugged. Good manners meant you did not make a fuss. And the flat seemed so different with the lights turned off and the curtains safety-pinned together and just the glow of the candles on the mantelpiece. Everyday life was smoothed away and in its place was a great nothingness. The blackness and blankness of the room snuffed out the wriggling white bodies on the floor, as though they were all already dead. Nothing mattered and no one had given Marie permission to leave and in the morning everyone would laugh at her for not enjoying herself. They wouldn't tell Floss, though, or Margaret, when they went back to work after the weekend. Those two would really draw the line at such antics. They wouldn't approve of capering about in your birthday suit and making mock. The goings-on would be carefully concealed from them.

Marie wished it was Monday morning and she was going in to work to be teased by Floss and hear Margaret complain about her daughter-in-law. So she decided to make the morning happen.

Annunciation

She stumbled out. She picked up her handbag and bumped down the stairs and into the street. If she kept running she wouldn't meet anyone and then there'd be no trouble. But she was wearing high heels and she tripped up and fell into a puddle and started crying, and Joe found her. He helped her up, held her arm gently, and walked her down Charing Cross Road. He took her into a pub.

The West End blazed with light. Marie was astonished. It was still evening, not the middle of the night at all. London was not dead and asleep but very much alive and shining, and the Soho pubs were still open, and men were sitting around smoking and reading the evening paper just as though they were in the normal world, having a pint and doing the crossword before going off to meet their friend. That was so comforting. Joe and Marie sat down in the saloon bar; they tucked themselves into a quiet corner. It was warm. Joe made Marie take off her shoes, crouched in front of her, and dried her wet stockinged feet with his handkerchief. It was a blue one, with a yellow paisley design. It felt very soft. He apologized for the streak of brown on one corner, where he'd been wiping a brush.

Joe had a creased, battered-looking face, thinning fair hair that flew up round his head. He had a wide smile. To gesticulate he pointed one long forefinger in the air. He bought Marie a gin and asked what had happened. She blurted something out, and he began laughing, as though she were actually quite dashing and witty, despite her laddered stockings and her broken heel and her tears. He coaxed out of her what the matter was, and he listened.

– You're mocking me, Marie sobbed.

– No, Joe said. It's the poster of the goat that's funny, not you.

He didn't try and come on to her in any way. So she started to like him, that quickly. She was grateful to him.

She had a second gin and tonic.

– Oh, I do love gin, she said.

The sharpness cut with sweetness, the bubbles of the tonic fizzing up her nose, the ice clinking against the side of the glass, the frosted lemon slice. She had a cigarette too. After a third gin and tonic she began to feel better. Her feet didn't feel so cold any more now that her stockinged toes were drying out in the

Michèle Roberts

warmth. Her face felt rosy again.

Joe told her about being an artist. He'd been to an opening in Cork Street earlier and was on his way home. Marie didn't know what an opening was but she nodded and pretended she did. She'd brightened up, begun to feel she belonged in the world, could see herself in the decorated mirror opposite, powdering her nose and applying fresh lipstick. She started enjoying the noise of jukebox music and chatter and the acrid smell of fag smoke. She'd come back to life because she had someone to talk to. She told him all about her evening classes.

Back in the street she threw her bunched stockings and her broken shoes into the gutter and walked barefoot. Joe bought fish and chips then hailed a taxi and took her back to his place. There was only one bed so Marie slept in it with him. He didn't try anything on. She couldn't believe it – how nice, how respectful, he was. Sunday morning he dug her out a pair of shoes from the back of a cupboard, old ones of his daughter's, brewed tea, grilled toast and kippers, went out and bought the papers. Sunday lunchtime they went to another Soho pub, a different one from the night before, and drank Bloody Marys. It was a French pub, apparently. Joe pointed out the silvery urn on the counter which dispensed water into your pastis, clouded sherbet-yellow to lemon. Marie tried pastis and loved the aniseed taste. There were lots of men there who all knew Joe. They dug him in the ribs and called him an old dog. Several of them insisted on kissing her hand. Then Joe escorted Marie to her flat. Having him with her made her feel bold. She didn't have to explain anything, just handed over a week's rent in lieu of notice. She packed her two suitcases. At Joe's she cooked supper: eggs and bacon and black pudding.

Monday she went into work as usual. Her ex-flatmates didn't say anything in front of Floss and Margaret, and neither did she. In the evening she went back to Joe's. An address near Mornington Crescent tube. A warehouse-like building that she thought at first was his flat but found out later was only his studio. Part of an ex-factory, near the railway lines out of Euston, that he shared with two other artists. He was on the ground floor and they were above. Walls of bare brick; an interior dedicated solely to painting, to the clutter and paraphernalia of work. To

49

Annunciation

Marie the smell of turps and gasfire fumes, the untidiness, was romantic and glamorous. She liked the way the space was not divided into separate rooms. The bed was up on a platform, and the bathroom was in the galley kitchen. You heaved a board over the bath and then you could stack the washing-up on it. There was a cold water sink, a small camping fridge, a two-ring Baby Belling, all packed in tight together. The toilet was out the back, in the yard.

It wasn't an accident, Marie's falling in love with Joe. The psychiatrist pointed that out. Though she was taken by surprise she helped to bring about her fall. She consented. She jumped into the free air and he caught her. One reason for her continuing obsession with him: he caught her and knew her.

– Stupid girl, he'd say to her very fondly: stupid girl.

He found her out – he recognized her fear. He sniffed it, forced her to confess to it. The first time he wanted sex with her she didn't come. Of course she didn't. He was fingering her too abruptly, impatiently waiting for her to heat up and be ready; instead she got jumpy and irritable. He was rubbing her too hard. When was this going to stop? Couldn't he just get on with it – enter her, fuck her, pant and gasp, flop on top of her, fall asleep? By now Marie did know how to make men come – you moved your hips in a certain way and that did for them; then they left you alone. In Joe's copy of *Lady Chatterley's Lover* the gamekeeper said doing that was a proof of hating men. Marie did think most of them were disgusting. She thought she was disgusting too, letting any of them come near her; she'd had that well drummed into her at school; and sometimes she thought Mum and Dad had been right; she didn't like those swollen cocks, as she explained to the psychiatrist, that had a life of their own and seemed little to do with the human beings they were attached to; there were far too many cocks in the world always popping out of men's trousers just when you were longing for a bit of peace, and she hated being nagged for not enjoying herself more. The psychiatrist agreed with the gamekeeper Mellors: he thought Marie was promiscuous and frigid; she hated men and wanted to castrate them. She was faking it: pretending to be a babe in the woods but really wanting to bite men's penises off. Long before she met Joe Marie had indeed learned to fake it, because that helped shorten the whole experience and you didn't get told off for not having come. She tried to fake it with Joe but he knew what she was up to and just laughed. So he got the power over her that way, knowing she'd lied, knowing she couldn't come, then showing her how to.

He tied Marie's hands and feet to the bedstead with silk scarves. His reasoning was that she had to be forced to enjoy herself, against her will. It worked. She did learn how to come that way, because however hard she begged him to stop touching her, he wouldn't. He forced her to tell him she didn't want to be rubbed but stroked. He learned how to do it properly and went on long enough. Once Marie'd come, he'd photograph her. Then he'd fuck her. Then he'd untie her. Sometimes he didn't fuck her at all, just tied her up and drew her or photographed her. The psychiatrist explained she wasn't just promiscuous and sadistic – she was masochistic as well. She let him do it. She stayed with him. Every night she went back to him; back for more.

Marie felt she mattered to Joe. He loved her. She nicknamed him the pirate; because of the way he had claimed her. He needed her and she inspired his work. He talked to her quite a lot when they were on their own, and she understood him, his hard childhood, why he was difficult, why he sometimes lost his temper and slapped her. She learned what not to say or do, to keep out of his way when he was in one of his moods. At least he had feelings. He wasn't cold, like her mum and dad. Most of the time he was charming, very funny and sweet. That's why she stayed with him, she told the psychiatrist – he was lovely company, in the main. He had a soul, and he made her feel she had one too.

He had to go and see his wife sometimes. He made that clear right from the start. When Marie came back from her job at night he would sometimes be there and sometimes not. She always cooked, in case he came in. Those nights when she was by herself she would drink beer and read books. She'd given up her evening classes, now she had him, but she still wanted to improve herself. So she read a lot. She read D.H. Lawrence and Albert Camus and T.S. Eliot. On Saturday afternoons, if Joe was visiting his family, she'd rummage in the second-hand bookshops in

Annunciation

Charing Cross Road and come home with a bagful of bargains. She'd go shopping in the market in Inverness Street for vegetables and meat. She was learning how to make dishes she'd never heard of before, like Boeuf Stroganoff and stuffed peppers and cassoulet.

Joe didn't take her with him when he went to the races or to jazz clubs with his friends, but she accompanied him to shows and openings. She dressed up for him on these occasions in her new outfits from Biba. The shop had just opened and the clothes were like nothing she'd ever seen. She bought a skinny mini dress in purple and another in orange paisley, with a low neck. A white jersey tunic and matching trousers, cut very lean. Tight armholes on the long, tight sleeves, edged with cloth-covered buttons, that ended in points coming down over the backs of your hands. The same buttons on the flyfront. She bought Biba make-up too: pale face powder, dark sludgy eyeshadow and vampy lipstick. False eyelashes and false fingernails. She showed off her long legs and her newly blonde hair.

– Beautiful chick, Joe said.

Marie stared at herself in the mirror, to find her beauty.

A face that was perfectly calm and blank, like one of Joe's canvases before he painted on it; huge eyes giving nothing away; a mouth that did not talk. Did beauty come from gleaming cheekbones, full lips? She wasn't certain that her beauty was hers. Where did it come from then? She lived just behind her beauty. Nobody knew what she was like underneath. That was her fault too, because she didn't tell them.

When they went out together there were rules. Marie had to be discreet, unpossessive, let Joe talk to people in peace, not claim his attention. It was a secret game they played on these occasions: not openly talking to one another; communicating only in their personal sign language. Sometimes, the posher the do the better, he'd pretend not to know her at all, and she'd pretend to have come in off the street and be trying to pick him up. He'd make her work quite hard to get his attention, and it had to be subtly done or he'd just turn his back and ignore her; she was never to approach him directly or break into a group of him and his friends. She could just hover and see what happened next.

Michèle Roberts

Eventually they all got to recognize her. They called her his floosie. She didn't mind because she was in love. Floosie-Maroosie was a happy girl.

The psychiatrist said patiently – so you had fantasies of being a prostitute?

Marie modelled for some of Joe's friends as well as for him. The ones who'd continued being figurative painters and not gone in for abstract work. They shouted at each other about this all the time in the pub; sometimes they got into fights, once they were drunk, and lugged each other out into the street where there was more space for punch-ups. She didn't talk to any of them much because they were all so brilliant; she never knew what to say. They wouldn't have wanted to talk to her anyway. It wasn't her place, to be talked to. She got drunk instead and then had a hangover next day and was late for work. Floosie-woozy. In the end, when the supervisor threatened her with the sack, she just walked out. She didn't say goodbye to anyone. She just went. Then she and Joe were in a pickle because of money being so short. She began modelling at art schools part-time, and took a waitressing job three days a week in a coffee-bar.

From time to time Joe sold a painting. A woman called Anne, whom he'd met at an opening and chatted up, had become first his patron and then his friend. In April of the year Marie moved into Joe's studio, Anne bought three of his drawings. He took Marie with him to deliver them and pick up the cheque. Anne lived in a shabby villa in Notting Hill. She was old enough to be a grandmother but she didn't look like one. Her black hair was done up in a chignon and she wore a short black silk dress and had fabulous legs. She screeched with laughter and called both Joe and Marie darling. At first Marie was nervous, even though by now she knew how to hold a knife, and to say lavatory, drawing-room, sofa, napkin and so on. She'd have been presentably quaint if she'd been a proper cockney but lower-middle class wasn't on. Another reason she kept her mouth shut in company and just looked beautiful. Upper-class people spot you immediately, she knew, whether you keep your mouth shut or not. You can't fool them for long. This woman saw through Marie immediately. Marie watched her sizing her up. Then she felt her being nice.

Annunciation

She drew Marie into the conversation, not with that kind of politeness that is like a slap round the face, terribly condescending even while they're pretending they aren't, but as though she liked her.

The room was all white, furnished with antique mirrors, fat white cushions on the white armchairs that you sank into, modern paintings on the walls. Marie felt as though she shouldn't breathe in case she dirtied something.

– Come on, darling, Anne said, have another glass of pop.

They drank two bottles of champagne. Anne wrote Joe his cheque.

– I'll give one of the drawings to my god-daughter Lizzie, she said, she's living in a commune in the East End. Could do with some brightening up.

Joe got up. He jerked his head at Marie – time to be off.

Anne put her hand on Joe's arm, looked him in the eye, and said – now just make sure you're kind to that little girl and don't do anything to hurt her.

Marie realized – she means me.

Suddenly she wanted to hurl herself at Anne; she wanted to sit in the armchair with her and have her put her arms around her; she wanted to lie in her lap like a baby; she feared she'd start crying and never stop.

She hurried out after Joe and didn't even say goodbye to her hostess, let alone thank her for the champagne. When they got home Joe slapped her for her bad manners. Afterwards he took her out for a Chinese meal.

Lots about Joe that Marie didn't know, even though she rummaged through his things when he was out, read any letters he left lying around, attempted to listen to his conversations on the telephone. She did discover that, contrary to what he'd told her, he was divorced, and that his children were grownup. He'd never wanted Marie to meet his kids. He'd kept her away from them. She assumed their affair had to be kept a secret because the children were so young.

Now she dared to ask him – so where do you go, then, on the nights you're not with me?

– Now you're beginning to sound like my wife, he told her, I love you because you never nag or whinge. Don't spoil it.

She began frying chips at the stove. He came up behind her, put his arms around her and pinched her nipples. Marie didn't dare wriggle out of his embrace lest in the struggle the pan tilted over and boiling fat splashed onto the gas flame and all over her.

– Tell me you were only joking, Joe said.

One night, soon after the visit to Anne, Marie got pissed at an opening and allowed herself to be chatted up by one of Joe's mates. They had a row in the street. Back at home he gave her a smack in the face. Next day, wearing dark glasses to hide her black eye, she went as usual to her job at the coffee-bar on Oxford Street. In her lunch hour she ran out to the chemist's near Portman Square to buy aspirin. She noticed, for the first time, the discreet sign on the building next door. Pregnancy Consultancy Service. Down into the damp, dingy basement she went, just on impulse, for a pregnancy test. The result was positive.

– How could you have let it happen? asked the psychiatrist, I thought you said you were on the Pill? I suppose you forgot a pill once or twice? That was careless, wasn't it? I suppose you thought you'd get him to marry you that way?

Marie protested – I haven't told him yet. I don't want him to know.

The psychiatrist said – thus denying him the chance to help you.

Marie went to Joe's GP, who refused to refer her for an abortion and scolded her for even considering one. She went to another GP, who told her she'd have to see a psychiatrist as well and see what he said. If they were both in agreement, then yes, Marie would get her abortion, on the grounds of being mentally unfit to become a mother.

Marie returned to the Pregnancy Consultancy Service, and discussed her situation with the trained counsellor. The other woman made it clear that here the doctors were sympathetic to women in distress and were likely to sign the relevant forms, giving permission, once the requisite medical examinations and interviews were gone through. Marie would have to pay, of course. And since she was more than twelve weeks gone, the procedure would be dilation and curettage rather than the

Annunciation

quicker and simpler vacuum method. The counsellor refused to advise Marie either way as to what she should do.

– That's not my job, she explained, that would be wrong of me. I can give you all the information you want but it's your decision. She sat implacably, twiddling her Biro, while Marie wept. Then she handed her a box of tissues.

– You ought to let the father know. It's only fair.

Marie told Joe the news that evening. She positioned herself near the door and watched him nervously. He began shouting. She scuttled out and barricaded herself in the lav, waiting until he had stormed off to the pub. Then she hurried back inside and looked through Joe's address-book for Anne's number. She couldn't have rung her parents. To them abortion was a mortal sin. It was Herod's Slaughter of the Innocents all over again, punished by an eternity in hellfire.

– Oh baby, Anne said.

Anne drove Marie over to the place where her god-daughter Lizzie lived. A communal household in Stepney, rented from a local landlord. All girls. Men came and went, but it was the girls' house. There was a room going spare, and Marie moved in.

Marie decided to keep the baby. She gave birth the following December, at the London Hospital. A gaggle of short-haired women, in greatcoats and boots, tramped in to visit her, bearing gifts.

Once the baby was brought home the household held a ceremony in the kitchen, to bless and welcome him. They encircled his head with a wreath of tinsel, hung fairy lights above his basket, lit candles for him, splashed drops of gin and tonic on his forehead, sang to him. Marie lit a cigarette and looked on, amused. Really, they were as bad as the Catholics, this lot. But at least they liked a drink. Today they were catering for all tastes. There was beer and cider as well as gin, a bottle of Veuve du Vernay, and herb tea for those who didn't booze. Marie cradled her son and looked into his violet eyes. He gripped her little finger in his fist and stared back.

The household had a cleaning rota, believed in sharing cooking and childcare. When they remembered to, Lizzie and the other women helped Marie in their cheerful, slapdash way.

Michèle Roberts

They took the baby out for airings in his pram, to give Marie a chance to catch up on her sleep, filled in forms for the DHSS, soaked and rinsed nappies for boiling.

Sometimes, when the baby woke at three or four a.m. and cried for a feed, Lizzie would hear him. She worked for the local Housing Co-op by day, and at night wrote poetry and stories, plays for her street theatre group to perform. She would creep out of her own room, peep round Marie's door. Marie, still half asleep, fumbling to fit the baby to her breast, would look up and nod – come in. Lizzie would perch on the end of the bed in the darkness. Then gradually she'd sprawl across the eiderdown, propped on one elbow. Sometimes they chatted; exchanged confidences. Often they remained in silence. Cool air blowing in from the gap at the top of the sash window, rattle of a distant train, murmur of lorries from the main road. The room held them. The baby gulped and burped. They swam in an ordinariness that felt safe, that let their edges blur and loosen. Sometimes they rolled up the paper blind so that they could see the stars through the black glass. Smell of warm cotton, the nappies airing in front of the gas fire, and milk. The three of them sat peacefully together, part of the London night.

image: toko
<toko.chan@virgin.net>

Aleksandar Hemon & Colum McCann On Writers and History

Colum McCann's new novel, Dancer, *tells the story of Rudolf Nureyev, beginning with the dancer as a six-year old boy in the Soviet Union at the end of the Second World War. Aleksandar Hemon's* Nowhere Man *tells, through various observers, parts of the life of Jozef Pronek, the Bosnian émigré character introduced in his collection* The Question of Bruno. *The fiction of both writers focuses on the personal experiences of characters trying to negotiate their immediate environments while simultaneously caught in the web of larger historical events beyond their control: the Second World War, the Cold War, wars in former Yugoslavia, the social disarray of post-Cold War USA. They sat down at their computers to discuss the roles that collective history and individual privacy, imagination and experience play in fiction, and also the function that writers and literature might perform in relation to politics and history.*

Douglas Cowie, Norwich 2003

Aleksandar (Sasha) Hemon: The beginning of *Dancer* is astonishing. You begin with a narrative that conveys the Soviet Army experience of World War Two. The subject of the narration is 'they' and the section ends by zooming in on a six-year old boy who's waiting for his father, one of 'them' – who could be *any* one of them – to come back from the war. This suggests that the boy's destiny (and the boy is, of course Rudolf Nureyev, the future dancer) is related to the collective experience you talk about. In a few pages, you gracefully move from a collective, historical experience to individual experience and the connection is not theoretical but emotional. What is the relation, in your mind,

On Writers and History

between the collective and the individual, between the historical and the private? And while we're at it, where do you think literature stands in relation to those categories? Is that relation a matter of research (as you'd obviously done a lot of research) or imagination or experience?

Colum McCann: The question of whether we write our own history, or whether history writes our story for us, is such a profound, prickly, confounding and even amusing one for the contemporary writer, isn't it? The job of 'fiction' (if such a word is apt and I'm not sure it is, I'd rather say 'story' or 'storyteller') is to imaginatively probe the small, anonymous corners of the human experience, where the untold has been relegated to darkness. But then there's the inescapable force of public events and history. The writer desires to see inside the dark corners in order to make sense of the room that has already been swept clean or clean-ish by historians, critics, and journalists. Poets do this too of course. A storywriter must be just as rooted as a poet in the way words sound, look, and bump up against one another. I don't see too much difference between the job of a poet and the job of the storywriter. Never have. Have you?

Sasha: No, I never have – for one thing, the poet and storywriter have no jobs, or they ought to have no jobs. (Have you ever read the transcripts of the trial of Joseph Brodsky in the Soviet Union? The main charge was 'parasitism.') But more importantly, poetry and 'fiction' (I'd rather say prose) are about language – they *are* language – as language is the main means of human interaction with the world, between one human being and another. Literature makes language reflect upon itself. This is not a matter of self-referential postmodern acrobatics. Rather, it's the *only* means available to *everybody* to access the collective human experience. Literature contains the history of human life from the times immemorial, one just has to read it (or listen to it). Of course, one can squander that incredible possibility and divorce literature from language, transform it into a marketable commodity, and sell it as a set of expert skills, while foregrounding 'the writer' as someone so exceptionally skillful

Aleksander (Sasha) Hemon & Colum McCann

and so attuned to his/her 'times' as to be a sort of a market-validated prophet.

Colum: I'm not quite sure what a collective historical experience is. Who would recognize such an experience? Would it recognize itself? I of course agree with you that everything is about language and that language itself is the collective human experience. The very fact of choosing a word (hopefully the right word) forces us into a place of privilege.

Sasha: Well, the collective Irish historic experience is what makes you Irish, for example – a history more legible to an Irish person than anybody else, something that defines someone as Irish, as opposed to English, let alone Bosnian. At the same time, at a certain level, there's a collective historic experience shared, not always kindly, by the Irish and the English – an experience that connects them, even if in conflict, and defines them against and with each other. And language is, of course, instrumental in defining, creating and recording such experience.

Colum: Patrick Kavanagh, the Irish poet, said that it seemed to him that the only valid violence is that which absolutely cannot be avoided. In the first half of the twentieth century, I'd think it's fair to say that the Irish were consciously using language as a tool, or a weapon, against the violence of the English. That language shifted and changed, of course. In recent years it's pretty clear that the more significant poets have come from the North. At the same time the position of the writer in the contemporary Republic (the South), while more public and acclaimed, is nowhere near as important as it used to be. It used to matter much more. Now very few people fear our bite. Much of what we do, I hate to say, is hidden and dampened, certainly when placed up against certain Irish writers of the past. In the present market it seems we drive ourselves further and further away from the language.

I think Kavanagh might have said the same thing about language as he said about violence: the valid word is that which cannot be avoided. Yet still we have to write from a mysterious, reckless place.

On Writers and History

Sasha: It's interesting that you make language a tool of struggle, indeed political struggle. Of course, the English used the language as a tool of oppression too. Many South Asian writers have used the same strategy. Was it Rushdie who coined the slogan 'The Empire writes back'? In the US a similar thing happens – immigrants transform the language of the host country, thereby appropriating it and using it as a tool of social and political struggle. It makes a lot of people nervous. Every once in a while I get a little lecture on the English language from a reviewer. My American wife, who is my first reader and editor, used to say, upon reading a 'weird' word or an unidiomatic sentence, she'd say: 'We don't say that.' And I'd say: 'Now we do.'

Colum: Which makes for a literature of immense variety and power and contention. Or at least potentially so.

Sasha: Here's a general, therefore questionable, statement: those in power work to preserve language, prevent any change, social or linguistic. Hence the drive toward 'realism' contingent upon the representational aspects of language, dependent on the fantasy that the language is as stable as the society, or at least it ought to be as stable as the society. Those disempowered work to transform the language and thereby change the condition of their existence in a society in which power has already been distributed. Language is constantly transformed in this struggle. William Carlos Williams, arguably the greatest American poet of the twentieth century, was once asked about a 'weird' idiom he had used in one of his poems. The interviewer asked him where he had got it. 'From our Polish mothers,' Williams said. It's in this that the political power of language and poetry lies – it shows the potential of social transformation.

Our insistence on language as *the thing* in literature logically leads to non-representational, or transformational, possibilities of creating literature, as opposed to the representational, pseudorealistically psychological modes of writing, dominating, alas, the contemporary Anglo-American literary production. So here's another reason why I admire *Dancer* so much: you chose a subject: dance – the body in space and time – which is perhaps the human activity least representable and reproducible in language. You forced yourself to find transformational possibilities of rendering dance in language. You forced yourself to write poetry. Was that a harder or an easier choice for you?

Colum: I suppose the storywriter has to follow that reckless inner need in order to go on a journey into an unreliable or perhaps undocumented area of the human experience. This is, in essence, transformational. To answer your question – in the case of dance, its aim is often to describe what seems otherwise indescribable. Finding a language to put on that was a terror for me. I mean, I was truly terrified. But it was also part of the challenge. I don't think anything exciting is ever achieved through predictability – it's like your last chapter in *Nowhere Man*, or the series of notes from Sarajevo in *The Question of Bruno*. The sheer beauty of surprise. For *Dancer* I started placing words together, choreographing them on the page until it seemed to me that they sounded right. And then I went to professional dancers and said, Will you listen to this please? I read it aloud to them. And then I asked – Does this sound like dance?

What attracted me about dance, though, was again, the violence of it. I mean, there's a tremendous violence committed on the body in order to achieve the appearance of ease.

Early on, when researching, I read in the biographies that Rudolph Nureyev's first public dance was at the age of six for the injured Russian soldiers who had been sent home from the front. What an image. A small blond boy dancing for men who had been through one of the century's most horrific experiences. Surely the story of these soldiers (their history, if you will) was just as important to the young Rudolph Nureyev as the fact that it was his first public dance. How can we tell the story of that dance without telling the story of the soldier?

As it turned out this was a fiction. I just found this out in the past few days. I was flabbergasted. Nureyev himself had created a fiction about dancing for the soliders. He lied. A biographer had taken it as fact. I took the 'fact' and tried to make a fiction of it. Which makes me think of the wonderful merry-go-round that we sit on . . . how often we get fucked off by a wooden horse into the waiting crowds.

On Writers and History

I often feel that we should try to write outside what we supposedly know, in terms of texture, in terms of reach. It's a huge task, of course, to write outside of what we know or don't know. Often it can make the storywriter into a megalomaniac of sorts: he has to try to distill the collective into the individual by attempting to override the accepted history. That's arrogant, I suppose. I mean, would you agree with me that writers are generally arrogant bastards? The idea that someone might want to read what you have written is a spectacular leap, isn't it? And yet – behind that – one must believe that, out of our arrogance, something selfless might emerge?

Sasha: You know what, I don't think that is arrogant: language belongs to me as much as anybody else. The hope that someone *might* want to read what you wrote is but a hope, and it is different in degree, but not in kind, to the hope that, when you speak, someone might hear you. Thinking that someone *should* or *must* read you is arrogant, and God knows that there are plenty of writers who like to complain about not being read enough.

Colum: Ah yes. The fact of writing is not necessarily arrogant, but the expectation behind it can be. That's an important, if not the defining, difference.

Sasha: This might be a sad fact (for 'the writer'), but 'the reader' doesn't owe a thing to 'the writer.' This is a simple way to put it: I write hoping that I could bear witness to history. And I don't mean the history of big events and great men – rather, the history of human experience, from the motes of dust floating in my room to genocide. It is a consequence of a need to participate in history, from which I – as a hastily assembled individual – am always excluded by the great fucking men and the powers that be. I see it as a matter of plain survival, rather than my job as a writer (or 'the writer') – I'm a writer only incidentally, because, in a way, I have no choice, it's a means of survival. But there's always a peril of slipping into a sort of historical solipsism – one of the things I find impressive about *Dancer* is that you extract someone else's life history from the history of crude facts. There's World War

Two and then there are women washing the wounded men. I've read a mountain of books about World War Two (for one reason or another), particularly about the Eastern front, but when that woman washes those soldiers I imagine understanding what it might have been like (and still we don't exactly know what *it* is). I came as close to knowing as you can without actually experiencing it. You rewrote history as life, recreated facts as experience.

Colum: I wrote that in a sort of blind haze: the idea of women washing the soldiers seemed to be 'in' the war and also 'away from' the war.

I think that history is often confined by the machinery of facts. But facts are mercenary things: they can be motherless, fatherless, sent to the orphanage to pack the cardboard boxes. This is where the storywriter comes in. Doctorow, in his essay 'False Documents', talks about the notion that a sentence composed from the imagination (as opposed to one with a strict reverence for fact) confers upon the writer a higher degree of perception, acuity and heightened awareness. He mentions novelists splitting themselves in two, 'creator and documentarian, teller and listener, conspiring to pass on the collective wisdom in its own language, disguised in its own enlightened bias, that of the factual world.'

A writer looks at the 'facts' and then tries to follow an obscure urge and see where it leads him or her. For me, reading about the war led me to this imaginative place where a woman was washing the soldiers. I don't know where she came from. I just read and read and read – booklets about winter warfare, poems from Russian writers, accepted histories, and then, when I went to Russia to research, I interviewed old men in military hospitals – and compacted it all into an imagined story that I hoped was honest and representative.

But my first instinct is to try and tell a good story with as many or as few words that suggest to me that it is 'right' or 'realized'. So it's facts, imagination and language all rolled into a tight but bouncing ball. And then of course we use the experience of our own lives to penetrate the gaps.

On Writers and History

John Berger, in a quote that's almost become a cliché because it's so perfect and apt for writers, says: 'Never again will a story be told as if it is the only one.'

Sasha: Yes, yes, I agree with you, by and large. But for the sake of our conversation, let me play a devil's cryptofascist advocate: why probe the small, anonymous corners of human experience? Why bother with unimportant experiences? If history is a history of man's greatness, why waste time on little things?

Colum: First of all history can't be a history of greatness: that almost seems like a logical impossibility, doesn't it? I mean, take one look at George Bush. Enough said. The story of the United States in 2003 would be far more poignant, intelligent, provocative and humanly useful if the writer, for example, told the story of the young migrant worker, or the dockworker, or the housewife, or any number of people whose stories are traditionally hijacked and relegated to the dumb-bin. I'm not talking (necessarily) about the working-class hero. I'm talking about the stories that, just for a moment, take your breath away and make you aware of the very fact of being alive.

Sasha: Yes, but George 'the Little' Bush is determining the ways in which the migrant worker experiences his/her life – they might get arrested and detained indefinitely, they might not be able to get a job, they might get fired so Cheney can pocket another million, they might be killed by one of the Ashcroft patriots masked as a lawman. So even if we agree that George Bush is but a petty, provincial, patriotic idiot, he can run this world into the ground, and it seems he's all too happy to be doing it. A story can take your breath away, but Bush can take your life away. What is it, if anything, that we can protect from him and other 'Great Men'? What is worth protecting? And how can literature protect it?

Colum: I think by telling the story of the migrant worker – how he gets kicked around, not to mention how he kicks others around – you are telling the story of the larger 'Great Men.' I don't mean this in the sense that it's diseased by self-consciousness. Books that are wrapped solely around ideas are doomed to failure. But I think that the small anonymous corner we're talking about is where most of us live our lives, and those things that Faulkner talked about – courage and honor and hope and pride and compassion and pity and sacrifice – are to be found in the small gesture, or the small life. These are things worth protecting. And literature can protect them by saying that they exist, they continue to exist and that they must exist. And not only that, because just saying they exist might be interpreted as a sort of passive critique: one must be prepared to say that these are not just individual stories, but stories relating to our larger nature, to the human condition. That each story has grand importance.

Sasha: I suppose you can tell the story of the migrant or a minimum-wage worker, by telling the story of those who skim the profit off their work. One story is never enough. I need to tell the story of my enemies to tell my own story.

Colum: Yes, and who legislates our lives? Who chooses to tell our story? Certainly Bush will never tell the story of the migrant worker. Bush wouldn't piss on him if he was on fire. Bush doesn't even believe that that story exists. It's only when the worker cuts through the barbed wire on Bush's ranch that he recognizes that someone's out there.

Sasha: The whole goddamn US of A is his ranch . . .

Colum: . . . and then he'll send his henchmen out to murder the 'intruder.' It's the writer's job to be contrary. It's the writer's job to cut that fence. This is one of the ways we can participate in history. The sad part of the matter is, however, that the contemporary writer is generally not seen as part of the political or social scene at all. He or she is not muzzled. I'm not favoring censorship of course but I am favoring anger. But, then again, the question is, is this our fault? Are we the ones to blame?

On Writers and History

Sasha: Yes, we are to blame, whoever *we* might be. What I think happened is that writers have been reduced (some would say promoted) to the status of expert professionals. We presumably possess the lofty skills of writing and those skills are valued by the market, for which we get rewarded by the reviews praising the skills, by academic creative-writing positions, by hefty advances. All you need to have to be a writer is such skills, which are – at least in the USA – easily acquirable through creative writing programs. Literature has been reduced to writing, writers have been relegated to irrelevant experts, while the price for being valued by the market is, of course, dehumanization and reification. The writer becomes a commodity, or, if he or she is lucky, a franchise – can anyone remember the last time John Updike, say, wrote anything relevant? He's in a cozy position in which he cannot possibly write anything relevant. Writers congratulate one another on skillful gimmicks and advances, all in the relative obscurity of the literary market and launch parties. You would be hard pressed to find a heated, passionate polemics between writers over some aesthetical, let alone political, issue – nobody seems to care enough, and many are scared to come off as pretentious. (Didn't *Granta* advertise itself a while ago as a magazine for the people who hate literature? God forbid *literature*. Writing is far less threatening and demanding – all you need to do is recognize an expert when you read his or her work. It's like recognizing a well-made piece of furniture.) To be heard at all I have to be validated as an expert professional, but the moment that happens all I can talk about is my (pseudo)expertise which is equal to all other modes of literary expertise valued by the market. Or possibly, there might be some interest in the 'autobiographical' aspects of my work, the understanding of which would lead to an understanding of the ineffable mystery of the expertise.

I crave substance – literature is the only thing I trust in this world, I need it to live and survive as a thinking, feeling being. Without it, I'm nothing, I'm nowhere. I despise the people who reduce literature to writing.

Colum: 'Without literature we're nothing, we're nowhere.'

What matters is that it matters. This is not just some coy little roundelay. Of course some might say this reeks of self-importance. Fine, fair enough. It IS self-important.

Sasha: But what about the storywriter's reckless need to obey and reinforce the dominant power structures? There was a large number of writers in the USSR who followed their inner need for power or, at least, sheer survival. What about the Western writers who mindlessly reproduce the bourgeois self and the spurious reality organized around it, which, needless to say, has direct political consequences? Who in other words is the storywriter you're talking about?

Colum: I'm thinking about people like John Berger who has known from the very beginning that freedom begins between the ears. That automatically we begin at a political place. I suppose the problem is that there are fewer and fewer writers like Berger. I'm not one to bitch and moan about the creative writing programs – I think they have their place – but increasingly what's happening is that we have all these mini MFA (Master of Fine Arts) novels that are mannered and housebroken. You go to university to learn the X, Y and Z of being a 'writer', and then you graduate, and your parents say, 'Well you're a writer now, son, go write'. And of course there are severe political and social consequences to this: we end up reinforcing the dominant structures. We have seen nothing and have had little time for rage or creative expansion.

Kerouac said that a writer should get out and chop boards and raise hell and never give a shit for all that dumb white machinery in the kitchen. I think most of us would admit that we'd rather read Kerouac than someone who sits on his arse moaning about publicity departments and advances all day long. And this chopping of boards and raising of hell is not necessarily a function of action – it can also be a function of the imagination. In other words we can achieve an altered consciousness within the language: we can do it within four small walls.

And I suppose the storywriter I'm talking about is the idealized version of self. The writer is you. The writer is John

On Writers and History

Berger, Anne Michaels, Michael Ondaatje, Edna O'Brien, Jim Harrison, Don DeLillo, Ciaran Carson, Donald Hays, Gabriel García Márquez, Frank McCourt, Peter Carey, Michael Cunningham . . . need I go on? The storywriter I'm talking about is the one who actually is aware that, although the stories have been told before, there is a deep need to tell them again.

Sasha: Yeah, but who does the writer function for? I like all those writers (and Vladimir Nabokov, Bruno Schulz, Danilo Kiš, Jorge Luis Borges, Emily Dickinson, Franz Kafka, W.G. Sebald, Nathan Englander, etc.), but they're all preaching to the choir, as it were. We all appreciate one another, inflate one another's importance, while the Bushmen of the world run the show. Why bother to write? Besides history competing with literature and the powers that be ignoring it, there's television (and its propaganda), there's film, complete with omnipotent special effects. There's the internet, something as close to the Borgesian superlibrary as we ever got. Not to mention that in the USA alone about fifty thousand literary titles are published every year, which is to say that a large number of books simply vanish. Why write stories? Why read books? Tell me.

Colum: I read books because people like Berger create stories that call the world into silence. I read his words with the sort of pleasure that I can't get from anything else and though it may sound sentimental, the world had changed as a result of having read them. So that, I'd say, is at least one good reason to read books – it can tilt the world in some tiny political, social or moral way, and, god knows, we certainly need some tilting. It's also the reason to write stories, wouldn't you say? Television and the internet don't compete. They don't call for difficulty (and all things excellent are generally as difficult as they are rare). Certainly on a personal level the television set doesn't have the power to tilt my own moral universe: except by the horrific reality of the news. Of course television reaches a far wider audience and that's a dilemma for the writer.

A lot of writing, I must agree, is done by this factory line of sick refrigerators: everyone working far too hard to be cool. The idea of the tortured writer speaking for the people? Come on. What about writers speaking *with* people? Literary life is pretty decorous these days. And so much is written with movie producers in mind, which is a significant clue as to what we think matters. When you tell people you write books they generally say, Oh. If you tell them you write movies they say, Oh really?

Apart from several significant exceptions (many of whom we've mentioned) it seems to me that there is a lot of blind timidity around. So many kitchens, divorce papers and café mochas. This sort of writing just doesn't interest me. Of course we get in trouble for saying these sort of things. People say, 'Who do you think you are? John Steinbeck or something?' Yes, I'd love to be Steinbeck, but I'm not. But I know that Steinbeck was socially engaged, that he brought public matters into private lives, that there was a political intent, even in the kitchens, and if he were around today he'd be thanking the stars for writers who are morally and politically at odds with the structures they examine: Gordimer, Márquez, Sebald, Saramago and so on.

And yes there are too many books being published. But so what? Every now and then a book will come along that will change us. There are two kinds of books, really – the good and the bad (there's ugly too, but let's not go there). In the end the democracy of time will leave the good ones standing. I really believe that. I suppose I have to. Otherwise I'd pack it in and take that job I was offered in L.A.

Sasha: You're right, but the assumption behind your (romantic?) hope is that the books will be read. But here you have Bush, a prime product of an alliterate culture, a hero of the fiction of benevolent capitalism, a priest of a languageless, mindless system of belief (rather than thought) – Bush is the exactly opposite of poetry, the enemy of language and thought. (Saddam and Bin Ladin and such are a thing of the past. They're on a history's garbage truck already, one way or another.) Now, I don't mean this to be an invective against the uncurious George (then again, why not), but rather to point at the fact that in the America and the world as imagined by Bush and those many he represents today, books are obsolete, not only unnecessary, but

On Writers and History

absolutely irrelevant. The Nazis hated books, but George & Co just don't give a damn. A book might change your world, but only the way painkillers change your world when you're in pain – they conceal the pain. And they work only for those in pain.

Colum: Heaping coals on one's own head is a pastime for saints – and then only up to a certain point. I don't believe in giving way to despondency. I agree with what you say about books being obsolete for people like Bush, but somehow that's all the more reason to write. There's occasion for a glimmer of hopeful rage here: maybe the novelist's opportunity is increased by the power of the regime to which he or she finds himself or herself opposed to. I'm not going to turn around and spend my life writing shit television shows just because I feel people aren't listening. There's too much power in language. There's too much at stake. Writing can operate beyond simply being an instrument of survival. I believe we must have a rage and a belief that it does matter. This is romantic, yes. But romanticism is equally as valid and possibly more productive than despondency. Put it like this: when the North of Ireland was being torn apart, limb by fucking limb, there were books being bought in the North, there were poems being written (Heaney, Longley, Carson, Muldoon were all writing political poems). I don't know if those poems went on to heal any of the wounds, but I have to believe that they helped, that the fact of their existence was a stay, even if an unrecognized one, against insanity. I advocate poets as Presidents but it'd be ridiculous – to be a poet you must engage in contradiction.

What was it like in Sarajevo? What was it like for you, being in Chicago, watching from afar? Did books matter then? I have to believe that you wrote *The Question of Bruno* from a direct rage about what was being done to, for and around your people?

Sasha: During the siege, Sarajevo had the liveliest, most passionate literary and cultural scene – people published books and put on plays and showed movies as symbolic acts of resistance in the face of Serbian fascism. These events were not just defiant acts of resisting destruction and cultural erasure, but they were communal activities, they reinforced the bonds between the people, while one of the goals of the Serbian fascism was precisely to sever those bonds. They were also, I understand, a consequence of a perpetual adrenalin rush, mainly caused by constant fear. It's generally agreed that the best literature in the Balkans came out of Sarajevo during and shortly after the war.

But it all fizzled out eventually – people went elsewhere, there was little money to do anything, and hopelessness, along with the sense of being abandoned by the world while the evil powers that be won, broke the back of many a Bosnian, writers included. Now it's hard to get a book published, and very few people read, kids are miseducated, there's no publishing industry, the library hasn't been rebuilt yet, but the internet is available. Last time I was in Sarajevo, I went to a cyber café to check my e-mail (being an addict) and the guy next to me was happily surfing bestiality sites, completely undisturbed by the presence of others around him. It wasn't even the crass, pathological impropriety of being aroused by raping beasts, but the fact that he felt he was perfectly alone. Sarajevo and its culture were complicated, rich social networks – you were *never* alone – but now many bonds have been severed. Literature was a matter of collective survival during the war, but it could not (logistically) sustain its relation to life after the war, because there is no social infrastructure to support it.

As for me, in Chicago, during the war (and thereafter), I read compulsively. I read the books I used to like before the war to see how they hold up in the face of the calamity, or, for that matter, in the face of my favorite literature professor, who became one of the top five nationalist Serbian leaders, which would have made him a war criminal, had he not shot himself. So some books I liked even more, but some of them I started hating intensely. I became less tolerant of bad books, of *idea* books and of 'writing.' I went to Chekhov to restore my belief in the possibility of human decency, but some books I threw against the wall and spat at them and took them to be a personal insult (the most battered one was *Best American Short Stories 1990*, edited by Richard Ford, another franchise writer). I still have a hard time reading contemporary literature, because most of it is merely writing, and often bad writing at that.

I concede that my disillusionment is probably due to my

On Writers and History

nearly pathological need for literature – I'm disillusioned because I believe in it and need it so much. Add to it my Bosnian, indeed Eastern European, experience. For many generations, my people have known that those in power could not care less about them and their little lives. Which leads me to this question: how much is your work determined by your 'Irish' experience? You wrote a book about a Russian/Tatar dancer. Did your Irishness matter either way?

Colum: Well, I'm an Irish writer. I'm also a New Yorker. I hold up these two contradictions and say that, finally, they don't contradict themselves at all. I suppose my Irishness, the plain fact of growing up there, contributed to my language and my sense of experience. Spending summers in Northern Ireland – hearing about my cousins being hauled off and strip-searched by British squaddies at the side of country roads – was an experience that outraged me, politicised me, though I didn't say anything about it for many years. I suppose it was going to London, at the age of eight, to meet my grandfather, who was a drunk, an Irish emigrant, lying half-dead in a nursing home, that made me think that writing could mean something. I walked in the door and he said: 'Ah, look, another fucking McCann.' But then I gave him a bottle of whiskey and two hundred cigarettes that my father had smuggled into the room. My grandfather sat by the pillow and he told me stories, about the War of Independence, the Irish Civil War. I can still, to this very day, remember the smell of him. It was awful and unforgettable – but has now become completely bearable in memory. I loved that moment. The next week, in school, in Dublin, I was given the assignment of writing about the person I most admired. Naturally I wrote about my grandfather. I was surprised there were people like him in the world. I'd grown up in the suburbs of Dublin. I'd never before gone to London. The fact that people like him were in my blood amazed me.

In addition, just the fact of learning Irish – it's not my native tongue, but I grew up learning it in school – was instructive. Irish is an altogether different tongue, complicated, onomatopoeic rather than descriptive, and oblique almost to the point of mystery. Meld this, then, with English, and you have quite a concoction. This mixture has all sorts of political and psychological consequences for the Irish writer. A big fat guy called Mulligan didn't just come down the stairs – rather, 'stately plump Buck Mulligan came from the stairhead, bearing a bowl of lather . . .'

We were colonized and we used language as a weapon to defeat our colonizers. Joyce and Beckett and Yeats and Wilde and Co took the language of the English and wrote it better than the English themselves. And so I grew up in a country where language is still revered and loved – though things are changing and Dublin is twinning itself psychologically with Disneyland these days. It's awful. But that's another story.

So my Irishness matters, yes, but I don't want to become a professional Irishman. There could be nothing more boring. Some people say I'm in exile from Ireland, but that's horseshit. I'm back all the time: both in reality and in my imagination. I don't think exile can exist for a writer these days (certainly self-imposed exile) as it did for writers like Beckett. How about you? How do you describe yourself now? Is this even a fair question?

Sasha: I don't describe myself, I write books to avoid describing myself. I think of myself as many people at the same time. I constantly have spy or actor fantasies, I love multiple personalities. When my agent was selling my first book, *The Question of Bruno*, way back when, she dined with some people in Europe who were convinced I didn't exist. This was exhilarating to me.

As for calling myself Bosnian, it's a political choice, a matter of loyalty to my friends and neighbors, and not an ontological or metaphysical or genetic situation.

My self is a compound self and definitely unstable. I have to live out all its fantastic possibilities in literature, reading and writing it. Literature is what keeps me together. First and foremost, I'm a writer/reader, everything else is secondary, one of the many identities. Perhaps that qualifies as some sort of psychological or psychiatric disorder: Literary Fanatic Syndrome or something.

On Writers and History

One of the earliest Jorge Luis Borges essays, written in 1922, is called 'The Nothingness of Personality.' In it, the blind poet says: 'There's no whole self. Any of life's present situations is seamless and sufficient . . . I, as I write this, am only a certainty that seeks out the words that are most apt to compel your attention. That proposition and a few muscular sensations, and the sight of limp branches that the trees place outside my window, constitute my current I.' Not only true, but beautiful.

Colum: So the trees 'place' the branches, and then the tree goes in search of a forest. I suppose I'd describe myself (as I have two kids and another en route) as a father/husband first and a writer/reader second. I like when Pasternak says that, despite all appearances, it takes a lot of volume to fill a life.

Sasha: It takes a lot of language to live a life.

Aleš Debeljak
Poetry

AN ÉMIGRÉ WRITER ON THE DRAGON BRIDGE

Open suitcases, it has sometimes been thought,
hide fates that are unknown to us:
from the hotel to the airport and beyond, through
centuries of wind all the way to the constellation Orion,
                                                travellers mince
carefully, searching in the rites of sleepy nations for
the consolation they can no longer get
from old photographs and books about the life
of their ancestors. An everyday
request could still become a prayer,
medicinal tea, the bitterness of endless explanations,
a language that refuses to yield to them,
scattered coins and suffocatingly low ceilings,
immensely large things that multiply
fear in little souls. A warmth that they all
remember will blow up from the south: for
everyone is guilty in the name of love, of course.
From the uncomfortable chairs in waiting rooms
and on the platforms they have but one desire
that rises quietly and is deceitful as the mist
over the railing that cracks beneath them. It groans and
lets them hang there for a second, why should they be an exception,
before floating off toward the tranquil river which swells
in the dry season, carrying suitcases and books
to the delta, to false consolation, to a poorly sung elegy.

Poetry

TO CHOSEN FRIENDS

Released by a child's hand a kite appears for a moment,
totally scarlet, above the herd of white cities and above
the fires. Come. Follow me now. It's not far
to a spot where you will get a good look
at ripened fruit lying on the wet ground as if
fulfilling a command. Unbearably necessary,
          like the horizon here that
checks the light and softens the defeats of human shadows.
You, too, will lie there. You are good at that. You'll count up
reconciliations with your neighbours,
         slips of your tongue, the horror
of deserting armies, the biography of castle walls,
          streets and squares,
spittle, your heartbeat and tensed nerves, some portraits
on murals, and, perhaps, supreme court documents.
Come. Follow me now. You will quiver, just as
I quiver in love and exertion: without memory
I survive fairly easily, though not without a legacy of juices.
I kneel alone for now, though I wouldn't want to do it forever:
Come. Follow me now. Kneel down before the family nest
and place your hope in wisdom that oozes thickly
from the gaping fruit. Come. Follow me now to a place where
nobody dares to go, for they exhale sweetly there or disappear
beyond the visible world in stammering and rain.

A LETTER HOME

I yearn for consolation, without bounds,
for forgotten caves where Bach
does not reach, for bells ringing plangently
across the monarchy that no globe reveals,
for the feverish concentration of hunters assiduously
caressing their guns, for the taste of tears I yearn,
for bubbling bone marrow, and for the miracle
that opens up like lips into a silent scream I yearn.

Aleš Debeljak

I alone pay heed, and in a second I respond
To the rhythm of tenderness down my spine, and I spring off,
as no one ever taught me, without bounds,
alone on a trail that's unknown to any brotherhood,
I follow the line of neck and head pushed backwards.
I give in to the inescapable command
that weighs on all my muscles and eventually forces
me to flower like a thousand sweet shots
and to begin to sing from the city
that is at once Rome, Medina, and Jerusalem, and
that consoles me as only one's homeland can.

Translated from the Slovenian by Andrew Wachtel

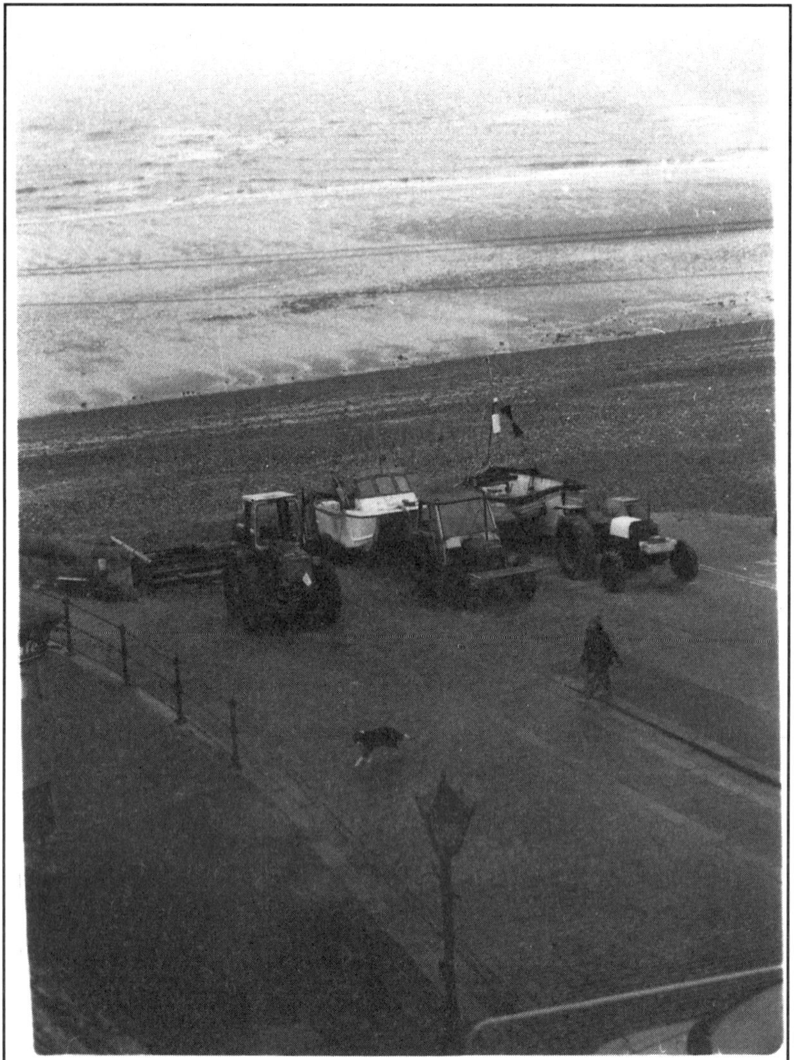

Semezdin Mehmedinović
This Door is Not an Exit

*'The door has no door, and yet – going outside
– I love both: the seen and the unseen.
Can everything wondrous and beautiful be upon
the earth – there – and yet the door has no door?
My prison cell accepts no light, except my own
inner light.'*
                               Mahmoud Darwish

I'll describe myself, my life and that means
My body in the world, with a picture that

Ushered in the war. The year was 1991.
In the glassed-in garden of the Writer's House

A peacock bumped into its reflection in the mirror,
                                              the bloody
Spot got bigger until it almost covered the reflection completely

Until someone sad enough separated the bird
                                              from the
Peacock's rage with a simple embrace –

Otherwise it *would* have killed itself, as surely as I would've

*

This Door is Not an Exit

It's already five years I've been tracking
This tree in front of the Voice of America building

Birds don't perch on its branches
And its leaves fall at the first

Autumn wind. Accompanied by the crowns and boughs
I've come to some concrete conclusions about myself

In the world. But the world
                            is neither
Better nor worse, and it can't learn

From what a tree sheds

                            *

In one of those parking lots in Mclean
I wait for her to finish shopping

She comes across the lot clutching
                            a paper bag
The birds flying up to the trees
                            in front of her –

Now she settles into the seat slowly
Putting the umbrella in her lap
                            like treasure

With no desire to free herself of its burden –
I look at her and the way she moves

Dwelling on the first signs of fatigue
– And for a second I feel like that umbrella
                            and all the rain in it

Bears the blame for all the unfulfilled dreams of youth

                            *

Semezdin Mehmedinović

In the garden of a restaurant a reddish coloured
Cat stares at tiny creatures in the leaves

Everything is so natural, that is, familiar
We sit around the cast iron table

Like a real family on an outing, and
I think of my father, he was a miner

In a coal mine, and I think of my
Father's father who was a miner

In a salt mine, I think of a black and white
Family photo from a time that makes me

Feel something like sorrow and not-sorrow,
Something from the glint of whose eyes

Only massive solar panels could make
Migrate into the language of poetry

Desolate February morning, I stumble
Upon myself in the room the phone isn't

Ringing, nor do I have anything to tell the world
I look at a painting on the wall, my portrait

Done by a painter from Sarajevo with a
New address and a Canadian
                                citizenship

I went out into the world to rest a
Body alarmed at the fear of disappearing

But courage left me at
                        the first gloom
Now I'm in the middle or at the end

This Door is Not an Exit

                it's all the same

Of a life that wasn't even indispensable
                *

I stop brooding as soon as I
Find a happy picture to amuse me

Mainly I find myself forgetting. I long
For beauty when life becomes

Completely unbearable. Everyone I
Know is like me. It seems we've come

A long way alone in sorrow only when
We're weary and it's then the grave of every
                one of us is in Palestine
                *

I never had a house of my own
Nor have I ever ceased imagining it –

– If I could have my pick, I point out,
That's what my house would look like

'But that's a Funeral Home' she says
And it's true, the kids use bright colours

To paint motifs of burial and death on the
Northern façade of the building –

And we drive on listlessly
The wind filling plastic bags

On the desolate treetops down
The whole length of Rhode Island St.
                *

Semezdin Mehmedinović

We had to stop and turn back at the front
Gate of the Harley Davidson factory

Disappointed. It wasn't, like they say, a
Work day. Just then a group
                        of bikers

Retraced the same path, whistling back
Towards the road and smiling all the while

They, apparently, had come home, to their
Place of birth, or death – it's all the same

But I, judging by everything, just went astray

Ramona and I fold sheets in the
Hotel laundry to the smallest fourths

And I flee the touch of her fingers
To avoid the jolt of an electric shock –

Ramona, you see, conducts electricity like the
Earth and she's got rings on every finger

But static electricity is a lightning bug
A synthetic lightning bug upon which

Warhol based an ominous ideology
                        materialized
By the metaphor of the world
                        as electric chair

*

This town's political, and we're nowhere to be found
Even though book writing, if you think of it as

This Door is Not an Exit

Metaphysical business, is political too –
Since I just got back

And there's a woman in the seat next to me
Reading *Love Letters from God*

The guy didn't take God on as a heretical
                                  pseudonym
Just someone in whose name he could give a little advice

A real bill of goods, an atheist manifesto
Hawked exactly like what it isn't

The woman had a sweater draped over her shoulders
And with her free hand, in the only data marking affection,
                                                   she wrapped it

Around her neck in an embrace

I'll never forget the woman
I saw at Clarendon Station

In an unnoticeable grey suit, an expression on her
Face that didn't reveal a shade of sorrow or a

Flicker of brightness, and now that she's gone
                              in the current of
Other bodies on the escalator

I can't even remember how she held her
Hands, she was so ordinary that

She seemed to appear here like a miracle
I'll never forget it: not the woman
But the way she presented herself

                                     *

Semezdin Mehmedinović

An expert on birdcalls
Who lives in Northern California

Claims that the same kind of bird sings
Different songs in different places

Which is a real anomaly
                              in dialect
In the winter he goes down to

Costa Rica to talk to the
California birds, to reconcile the

Kind of sorrow you feel away from home
I can't say I'm too happy about his gift

Because I think the most you can strive for is silence
Since I know nothing can reconcile the

Sorrow of exile from the grief
      of telling the dialects
Of southern slavs apart

                              *

I only saw the little African chimp
In Sarajevo once in the

Twilight of ninety-two
I was the only one on the main

Drag, and the trolley cables that tumbled
In the wind were grinding the asphalt when

I noticed an animal at a window above me
Pushing at the glass with his furry body
I couldn't believe what I was seeing
I was sure I was already dead

This Door is Not an Exit

and didn't know it

And that I'd gone over to the other side
Where borders between continents
                don't exist

                *

Yes, I used to hang out with some
Real desperadoes in those days

The world around feigned a
                mortal threat
And everything commenced in silence

I was under no obligation to speak –
The tidy world always invited

Me to, but only of what it
                wanted to hear
And the thoughts I had in me weren't mine –

So I kept quiet, I can now say, completely at ease
There where the only sure thing was death

                *

While I'm reading my stuff about the war
Gerard Malanga closes his eyes in the front row

Sub-consciously, since he worked
                with Warhol
In the Factory. He's gathered data on the crimes

Committed against the Bosnian people with the
Precision of final Judgement

Semezdin Mehmedinović

Gerard Malanga. In the front row seat, eyes shut,
Blind as the encyclopedia of crime

*

I don't bear the sorrow of a people within me
                                          but I know it

And I can't change anything in the world
                                         since I'm scared

Of even sounds I can't recognize in the empty halls at the
Voice of America: dozens of Japanese slippers brush the floor

When from the very end of the hall the smiling Dalai
Lama and a hundred Tibetans pop out before me

*

I always answer differently when it comes to the question
                                             of going back
I have nothing to complain about now that I'm here, but

I can't really reconcile myself with getting old and the
Picture I have of myself looking for advice on
                                       americanhearth.com

Whose photo exhibits I visit regularly at the
Editorial offices of National Geographic

The older I get, the less pictures of other worlds
Mean to me, tonight

She fell asleep with the TV on and a
Comb in her hair, I took a picture of it

And I'm still taken by the enthusiasm of a man
Whose whole world is made by leaning

This Door is Not an Exit

on one woman

I am, in fact, where you are, to make
Your weariness inspire meaning

*

At the fish market on the Potomac I think of my
American friends, their parents and grandparents

Who left Central Europe for good going to Mexico City
Buenos Aires or New York, thinking of my

Young American friends, I was convinced that the
World I know came into being with the fall of the

Austro-Hungarian empire, and with that discovery
I saw the market like the opposite of fish and cat –

Then I saw the Potomac, and yachts in the Marina

*

These are lines from a poem by Mahmoud Darwish: *I am an exile. / (...) Take me like a toy, a brick from the wall of your house / So our children will remember to return.* For days my son has been walking around the houses of Alexandria and taking pictures of doors. We've never had a house, which means that he's been an exile since the day he was born: already an immigrant twenty years.

I understand why he's got a habit of collecting doors, but I'm not very happy confronting it – I only really got drawn in to his work when, amongst all the doors he shot, he showed me this one:

Semezdin Mehmedinović

image: Harun – This door is not an exit, 2001

(FOR AMMIEL)

The sun went down right
        to the gas pumps

Then lost itself in the clouds
I'm standing on Telegraph Avenue and looking

Up, Czeslaw Milosz lives on the hill
And because of him I think of my
              room in Sarajevo

And I think of that room's bookish utopia
I had wanted to show the symbols of Islam

In the light of so-called western metaphysics
And I wanted to renew the forgotten

This Door is Not an Exit

Notion of Jesus the
          boy wonder
But it all ends in pure desire

As I'm standing on Telegraph Avenue now
I feel like I'm ready, because

There's nothing else I want to possess

Ben Faccini
Mokattam

Tonight, on the outskirts of Cairo, I watched a whole garbage village sing to the headlights of cars bumping over piles of refuse. A garbage collector's daughter had arrived back from her wedding. A loose ribbon of women shielded her as she moved up the streets of makeshift houses. Cars followed and hooted, wheels gliding in unison, sinking into bottle lids, paper and plastic. From the wound-down windows, the bride's family stretched out their hands to touch children running faster and faster. At the front of the procession, the occasional shimmer of white dress appeared in the mass of fussing arms. A bonfire was lit in the middle of the street, spreading and feeding off the waste around it. At around ten o'clock, the bride and groom were led away and ushered into a house at the top of the street. The crowd surged after them only to be met by a closed door. The beating of drums and clapping grew louder and louder. Men danced, twisting and pounding the rubbish as they turned. Then, briefly, there was a lull in the noise.

I sat on the bonnet of a parked car, looking down onto Cairo. The bonfire was sending paper transparent with flames into the air. In the distance, the centre of the city was a fragmented plate of light. Strips of melted rubber and gauze stuck to my feet as I left. The sound of the drums and the orange haze of the bonfire had gone by the time I reached the far corner of the slum. I had to return to the hotel to ring you. I tried calling you last night and the night before. The hotel receptionist told me it was the best time to get through to Europe. I let the phone ring at least twenty times before giving up. I can't believe I still haven't

Mokattam

managed to find you at home in the two weeks I've been in Egypt. Maybe it's better to write anyway. Somehow, I knew I'd be writing to you tonight and telling you all this.

You may wonder what I was doing in some garbage village when you thought me at our consulate and embassy. I did go to the Italian consulate and I was allowed to look through the archives for the day, but my work isn't progressing. There's very little left of the Italians who lived here at the turn of the century. In Alexandria, it was the same story. They show you the old Italian Club or a decaying house, nothing that I can base my research on. It's a shame, there is so much on the Greeks, but almost nothing original on the Italians. It's all very tiring and makes me feel I should have done this book years ago when I had more energy.

In any case, other things have happened. How can I say this? Two days ago, here in Cairo, in the hotel in Zamalek, I carelessly put my ring, your ring, on the side of the table by the television. I know I shouldn't have taken it off, but I did. My hands were swelling and itching in the heat and it felt uncomfortable. I must have forgotten to put it back on. By the following evening, it was gone. I searched the whole room for it, looking under the cupboard, behind the curtains. I turned my suitcase inside out and stripped the sheets off the bed. I even pulled up the edges of the fitted carpet. The hotel manager assured me that the chambermaids were honest and I believed him. I could only think that the ring had fallen off the table into the bin below which is emptied every morning. I enquired at reception. I was told all the hotel's rubbish was taken by the garbage collectors who service the building. I felt totally sick with panic. I couldn't concentrate on anything, let alone sleep. I thought about calling you there and then, in the middle of the night, although I knew you'd be upset. I sat up and watched television, unable to focus on my notes or even the bedside collection of hotel brochures and guides. Instinctively, I kept on feeling my finger, as if I had only imagined the whole thing. At five in the morning, I showered, dressed and started searching the room again, all to no avail. It's inexplicable. I still don't understand how it could have happened.

The night porter, who was still in the lobby as dawn rose, didn't know how to contact the garbage men or when exactly they turned up to collect the rubbish, so I had to wait for them myself, at the rear entrance of the hotel, next to the bins. The *zabbaleen* arrived with their donkey carts already half-loaded. Of course, I couldn't explain my problem except in the most basic of finger gestures which they almost misunderstood as obscene. Finally, they beckoned me onto a cart and I climbed on thinking their workshops were round the corner. Instead, we headed off across Cairo, with everyone staring at me in my suit and tie (I had wanted to go to the consulate again), propped up against huge stinking bags of rubbish. Near the *Al Qala* citadel, we veered off the tarmac road and started climbing some steep and narrow alleyways. Children appeared almost spontaneously. They stopped and pointed. From the pieces of metal and iron in the back, I had reckoned we were first going to some foundry, but we seemed to be moving into a slum: an imprecise pattern of uneven streets, parked trucks piled high with waste, donkeys tied up, all on top of the garbage. It was everywhere, the rubbish, a blanket on the ground, knee-deep in some places, clogging the alleyways. This was *Mokattam*, I was told, Cairo's garbage village.

Every street corner had a pile of smouldering refuse, each giving off its own particular stench of burning rubber and molten plastic. I jumped down from the cart. The drivers unloaded the metal at the back of a building. Inside, women and girls were squatting, sorting refuse into neat piles, cardboard to one side and cloth to another, tin in a corner, mineral bottles in another. Their bare hands were cut and swollen, working as fast as any machine. On the wall behind them, a colourful holy icon stood out, sparkling clean, as though the foul smells and filth could never touch it. Organic matter, animal bones and rotting vegetables, was being scooped up by a boy and thrown into the back of a low donkey cart. I tried to give my drivers some help. Each time I took a piece of metal, they removed it from me, laughing kindly and walking carefully round me to dump it on the heap on the ground.

Eventually, one of the men led me down a passageway stacked with so many mounds of different plastic that it had become a tunnel of bottled light. We came into a clearing hemmed in by

Mokattam

large cubes of compacted soft-drink tins. In front of us was a deep pit containing a fermenting mountain of peat-coloured compost. Children with carts were racing each other towards the ditch, their donkeys' hooves skidding and sliding down the final wooden ramp. They emptied their loads with impressive speed and then headed off again, uphill. At the edge of the pit was a white building, amazingly white. A woman came forward and welcomed me inside. She spoke quite good English and I explained my predicament, calmly, trying not to display too much alarm or confusion. It seemed she had already been notified of my situation. In a soft voice, she informed me that *Mokattam* covered a wide area and that I was already lucky to have found the men who worked my street. The rubbish from the hotel, though, didn't always stay with one family and the chances of finding a ring, unfortunately, weren't like those of recovering a piece of furniture or even a book. 'What did the ring look like?' she asked and, as I explained that it was a small gold ring with some faded initials on it, the futility of my search became all the more apparent. I tried to clear my head by observing the young women and girls around me as they separated out discarded cloth and bright textile cuttings to weave carpets. From a side room, I could hear the repetitive slam of wooden looms at work. Multicoloured blankets and covers were being stitched, delicate shapes and designs etched onto recycled paper. It was as though all the rubbish in Cairo was gently travelling downhill in a flow, ending up polished and purified in this white building.

I kept on thinking of your mother and how she'd given you your father's ring to keep for the day you married. How come you only told me a few years ago that your mother took it off him the day he died? Sometimes, you know, I felt it was too intimate, your dead father's ring on my hand, like the years of his life were closed round my finger. Every time I see your mother, she still takes my hand and holds it tight, too tight, to feel the ring against the softness of her palms. All this I explained to the English-speaking woman in *Mokattam*. I was entrusted with a new guide, a young man in a cap, about twenty years old. His English wasn't good, but he wanted to help. It was he who took me to the wedding

Ben Faccini

celebration later. We left the white building and turned down the hill. The soles of my shoes descended deeper into a sagging carpet of plastic bags and cardboard. I kept on looking round me in amazement at the industriousness of these people, shying away, only once, from a putrid alleyway strewn with syringes, soiled bandages and pill boxes. This area, the young man explained, was run by the families who collect hospital waste. Further down, a different street was crammed with pieces of car tyre, dissected and remoulded into black bales of rubber. Behind walls and corrugated iron pens, I could hear the noise of chickens and goats digging, rooting around in their own piles of waste. I had secretly begun to wish so many things. How, perhaps, here, in the dirt and filth of an animal pen, in the ashes of a fire, our ring would miraculously turn up. I kept on praying for a jubilant cry from one of the passageways and then the sight of a child running towards me with the ring held tight in its hand. My guide told me that a garbage collector had once been sorting out the rubbish in the bottom of his house and found a shattered watch with exquisite Roman numerals. He kept it nailed to the wall by his bed. Another had discovered a framed photograph of a wooden house and never given up hope of finding it, fixing it to his truck dashboard when travelling round the city. Many people in Cairo, the young man said, sadly believe the *zabbaleen* only live this way in the hope of one day making off with some rich person's absently-discarded valuables. I could only feel total admiration for these impoverished and resilient families who transform all this rubbish in a constant cycle of invention and renewal. If you could have seen the devotion threaded into the carpets, the colours breaking out of the young women's hands.

I met up again with the collectors from my morning cart ride. They were sitting in a large yard choked with litter. Much of it seemed to come from my hotel. There was an old menu from the restaurant, a ripped cushion cover from the lobby and tissues and half-cooked food. The men promised they would keep an eye out for our ring. I stood there, eagerly, for nearly three hours watching them sort and select the rubbish, but I could see from the thickness of the waste, on top of more waste from the day before and, probably, the week before, that the task was almost

Mokattam

impossible. I found myself checking under my feet, asking to turn over wads of cardboard, flicking blackened pieces of cotton wool to one side. I could feel the panic of the night before returning, the bareness of my finger again awkward and unnatural. If I hadn't been worried about upsetting the men next to me, I would have sifted and sieved every piece of rubbish in that place myself. It became unbearable just imagining that the ring was, perhaps, in that yard, somewhere, right under my feet, tucked inside the folds of a rag or a shredded newspaper. That's when I first heard the sound of singing and almost fled, with my guide, to listen. I spotted the corner of a wedding dress in the street above. We decided to follow the gathering crowd. More and more people were leaving their homes, pushing into the unpaved streets. By then, I think, people were getting used to the sight of me, wandering around, cutting my own little path through the waste, stepping over the stagnant potholes of oil and grime. They all knew I was the Italian after his lost ring.

It was night by the time the wedding procession reached its final destination. As the young married couple were led into their house, it became clear to me that our lost ring was somehow a gift to them, that if it was never found, it would stay deep in this layered soil, inside a carpet or crushed under a cart, but remain here, forever, in this garbage village. Maybe this won't make sense to you and I should be apologizing for the loss of your father's ring, but I gave up searching. I so wanted you to be with me. I wanted us to let go of this ring together, abandon it to the earth and this new regenerating life. At the citadel, I took a taxi back into the centre of Cairo. The lit-up billboards shone blinding colours into the car. The driver offered me cigarette after cigarette to break the silence and gridlock of the traffic. He dropped me near a junction and I crossed over the Nile towards the hotel, stopping to lean over the bridge. Faded plastic bags floated beneath me, whiteness torn and drifting. I knew I was looking for you on the water and I hid my face in the darkness because I saw that I was still your groom, a solitary groom, with my promises far behind me.

Ben Faccini

THE ZABBALEEN

The *zabbaleen* of Cairo are the descendants of Coptic Christian subsistence farmers who started emigrating from Upper Egypt in the 1940s. Arriving in Cairo in successive waves, they built shacks for themselves on the outskirts of the capital city, but kept being moved on for illegally occupying land. They finally regrouped under the cliffs and quarries in *Mokattam*, next to Cairo's citadel, *Al Qala*. Although the *zabbaleen* had finally found a refuge, their waste-collecting activities and their secluded location quickly cut them off from society. For many Egyptians, *Mokattam* became synonymous with squalor and poverty.

The *zabbaleen* set out early every morning onto the streets of Cairo, the women and girls staying behind to wait for the first piles of refuse to come in. Each family has a precise route through the city and a particular recycling specialization which can range from anything from glass, cloth and black plastic bags to mineral water bottles, tin cans, and animal bones. Families aim to service middle-class areas as they are more likely to generate the greatest amount of edible refuse for their animals and hold larger quantities of recyclable material. Once the refuse is collected, it is driven back across the congested, sprawling city up to *Mokattam*, a tortuous journey that is even longer for the poorest families who still use donkey carts. Recuperated material is transformed through a remarkably efficient range of methods. Plastic is made into bowls, coat hangers, shopping bags and floor mats. Cloth is washed, shredded and ground to produce stuffing for mattresses and cushions. Textile trimmings and fabric are woven into carpets, quilts and bags. Organic waste is fermented to make compost to sell to farmers working in the Nile Delta or for reclaiming desert land.

Tools are limited, conditions often risky and disease common, but the *zabbaleen* collect an estimated 3,000 tons of garbage every day and up to 85 per cent of that waste is recycled by them. Today, around sixty thousand people, directly or indirectly, live off this processing trade. Over the years, several Egyptian non-governmental organisations have introduced vaccination, hygiene and basic education schemes into the area, improving conditions

Mokattam

vastly. Once described as a vision of Dante's *Inferno*, *Mokattam* now has schools, a training centre, workshops and numerous small flourishing businesses. Many young *zabbaleen* have become entrepreneurs skilled in the art and chemistry of recycling, taking their expertise as far afield as the Red Sea, to the growing South Sinai resorts where the build-up of unprecedented waste risks destroying the fragile coastline habitat.

In 2003, the Cairo governor decided to hand the waste management of the city over to three foreign companies who intend to landfill the garbage they collect. The zabbaleen and their families may be left without their livelihoods and the knowledge of their recycling innovations and traditions lost with them.

Stef Pixner
Hah!

The summer you were ten Izzy wore a long black coat all through the hot green days of August. Round his grimy neck and face he wore a navy wool balaclava and he edged slowly along the road like a giant crow. You could see him come wobbling out of the vanishing point half a mile away down your long tree lined street. Sometimes you'd slip behind a wall or some dustbins hoping he hadn't seen you in case he hooked his arm in yours, saying walk with me, just a little way.

One day when you were on your way to the shops you couldn't avoid him and he hooked his arm through yours, holding you at his snail's pace past the chemist's, the post office, the greengrocer's, the pub, the dairy and the funeral director's, all the way to the bank. You stood next to him in the queue while he got a lot of money out in big notes which he put in a black and white striped plastic bag with red writing on. He asked you to tie a knot in it. Then he hooked his black clad bones through yours again and leaned on you hard as if he wanted to hurt you and every hot step along the long sun-speckled street to the house was agony.

In the big house, your family had the small top rooms where servants had once lived. Izzy had the great big drawing room on the ground floor which swept from front to back. You wondered why people had needed such a big room to do drawing in, and whether people were very different long ago. You guessed they must have been. Above Izzy lived Isla, who was Scottish, and her dog, and below him lived some students, but he thought the whole place was his. He used to wander into people's rooms when they were out. Or even sometimes when they were in, when they

Hah!

were sleeping, or getting their clothes on. So now there were locks on every door, like in a prison.

On the long hot trek home Izzy stopped twice, leaning on you even more heavily while he stood still and you breathed in his thick unwashed smell. He'd gone very yellow in the last few weeks and very thin. When you got to the house at last, dying of thirst, he asked you in to change a light bulb.

While you were up the stepladder fiddling with the bayonet fixing, Izzy got out his Bible and began to read you the story of Jacob and Esau. He liked that story. He liked the bit where Esau got betrayed by his brother Jacob and lost his birthright and his father's blessing. He read it over and over again and tears crept into his voice which made you think of the tap upstairs dripping into your stone sink. The ceiling of the drawing room was very high. From there you could see all Izzy's things, from when he was a trader in things. A stuffed bear six foot high with a leer on its face. A balsa wood palace from the far east in a glass case. Three big navy-coloured prams. He could see your things, too, when he came over to the bottom of the ladder with the Bible in his hand and leaned on it and looked up.

Izzy said will you promise me something Lily? You were stretched up as high as you could tiptoeing on the top of the ladder to put the fixing into the holder. Izzy said will you promise you won't let Moses Milion get hold of my money when I die? Izzy was at the bottom of the ladder looking up. You broke out in a sweat. You said my mum will be wondering where I am, can I go now Mr Mordecai?

As you skimmed up the stairs afterwards the front doorbell went. It was Moses Milion himself. Israel! you heard Moses say. How nice to see you!

A few days later there was a note for you on the hall stand in pencil on a torn piece of cardboard. *Dear Lily, I am awfully sorry to trouble you, but would it be possible if you could manage to buy me a pint bottle of sterilized milk, if you please and a small cut sliced bread, a small bread, as a large one gets mouldy in this warm weather. I shall be in all the morning. & Oblige, Israel Mordecai.* When you got back with the bread and the milk Izzy picked up his purse. He threw a

Stef Pixner

threepenny piece down under the table with a sly sideways throw. I've just dropped a threepenny piece, he said, would you be such a kind girl and pick it up for me. But it had landed under some junk he had under there, in among dead matches, milk bottle tops and broken-off pieces of cheese. You'd've had to've gone right down on your hands and knees to find it, with your bottom in the air. I can't get that for you Mr Mordecai you said, I can't see where it's gone, and you ran.

Moses came in again just as you went upstairs. You watched what went on from the top of the first flight, by the door to Isla's bathroom. This time Izzy said go away, in a cross voice, I'm too busy for visitors. He'd only opened the door a crack just to see who it was, the gas man maybe, or a parcel, but Moses pushed past him saying have you been to the doctor recently, Israel? You look a lousy colour. Moses was much younger than Izzy, shorter, broad, and he had a ruddy face.

Your mother said what's wrong with you this week, you've gone very quiet, but you didn't tell her because there was a feeling of shame like soap in your mouth. You didn't tell her either how you'd gone off God because you were on Esau's side. You knew your mother believed even though she didn't go to synagogue because she'd been talking to God recently. Oh God, oh God, please help me God. That's how you knew she wouldn't understand about how bad it was about Esau having been cheated. You thought more about such things these days. You'd noticed recently how being ten was different to nine because you saw into things, like your mother and father for example, how they cut each other with their eyes. Before, you'd thought all wrongs could be righted, but now you weren't so sure.

The next morning you were woken by a smell. It was the most terrible smell you had ever smelled in your life. It was like a hundred bad eggs. Sewers, sick, rotten cabbage and worse. Izzy had done a mighty number two and it came wafting all the way up the stairs and under your door. Even under the bedclothes there was no escape. It had got into your nostrils and found itself a home.

When you crept down the stairs later you found a note on the hall stand on the inside of a flattened out packet of tea. *Dear Lily,*

Hah!

I have a very important message for you and I shall be pleased if you could call in my kitchen before you go out this morning. I promise not to keep you more than 2 seconds. & Oblige Yours sincerely Israel Mordecai P. S. I shall be in all the morning. Thank You! You closed the front door as quietly as you could and ran off up the long street to see if your friend Becky could play out.

It was hours later when you got back. You put your key in the lock and heard voices. You heard Izzy shouting in a high voice but without the strength to shout.

You stole her! Go away! You stole her! he shouted. Moses was saying, loudly, I *married* her, Israel, that's all. You'll sign in the end, you know. You can't keep this up forever. Just then Isla arrived at the front door with her dog who was called Laddy even though it was a girl. This was because the boy dog Laddy had died and Isla had got another one the same only it was a girl, a small one with hair over its eyes. You said to Isla can I come with you to the park? She said OK lass and off you went, the three of you, and when you came back there was nobody about, just silence in the hall.

As you fell asleep that night you wondered where Izzy had put the plastic bag with the knot in it. You hoped he had hidden it somewhere clever like under a floorboard or stuck in a book.

Two days later the smell was worse. Bowel cancer, said Isla, who was sweeping the stairs when you went down in your slippers to get the post. She was in a nylon outfit that protected her clothes from the dust which clouded up, and sweeping like someone in a hurry. Isla did everything very fast. She made you think of something under pressure coming out of a nozzle. The only time she wasn't moving fast was when the two of you were sat either side of her gas fire with a cup of tea and she had a fag burning and Laddy lay spreadeagled out on the floor between you. Once she told you how she'd lived in the house thirty years and had known Izzy when he was middle-aged and had lived there with his sister. He was different then. He dressed very smart and had lots of girlfriends but never stuck with any of them,

When you got to the bottom of the stairs, there was another note for you. It said *Dear Lily, Firstly I thank you for what you have*

Stef Pixner

done for me, and I appreciate it, but I notice that you avoid me every time. For example, you come down very quietly, but before I go to the street door to speak to you very privately you seem to be too far away. Therefore I am obliged to write to you. I wish to speak to you about a very private matter. Yours Truly, I Mordecai. P. S. I will be in all the morning!

You went straight upstairs again and did a lot of things that surprised your mother, like, you made your bed and and put your shoes away. Also you cleaned out the guinea pigs. When you couldn't think of anything more to do you went and stood outside Izzy's kitchen door. Your heart was thumping. The door had layers of paint on it, the top colours chipped off and the bottom colours showing through. You could hear Isla. She was scrubbing now, a brisk swishy bangy noise where the brush head hit the stair edges, getting closer as she worked from top to bottom. You took a big breath and opened the door.

The smell gripped your throat and the floor was sticky under your feet. Izzy was sitting at his kitchen table. He had his stained longjohns in a wrinkled pile round his ankles, and a net curtain thrown across his private parts. His pale legs were blue-veined. On top of the balaclava was a gentlemanly trilby and the sun in the tall window behind him made a halo round his hat. You thought that without his long coat he looked more like a sparrow than a crow. On the table was an old biscuit tin with a picture of the King who'd abdicated on the top. Isla had told you how they'd done all the coronation mugs and tea boxes before he'd given everything up to marry a divorced woman at the last minute.

Open it, Izzy said. You thought the money would be inside, but all there was in it was a pack of playing cards and some curls of dark hair, a lipstick and a sea shell.

He said, they're hers. You said, whose? He said, Lily, do you love your sister? No, Mr Mordecai, you said. You should, he said. You would if she was drowned. I had a sister once, he said. She was stolen by a Zionist fanatic. Zionists! said Izzy. Robbers and fanatics! Promised Land! Hah! He looked on his table for something, pushing a pile of paper this way and then that way, fishing out bills with tea stains on them until he found a small square photo which he handed to you of a girl with dark hair and a dark dress, and said, Dolly. Even you could tell you looked like

Hah!

her. Suddenly you felt the life rushing in your ears, so loud you felt deafened by it.

You wanted something to say after that. So you said, d'you want a game of snap, Mr Mordecai? Izzy looked at you as if he'd never seen you in his life before, for such a long time you began to fidget. You noticed that Isla's banging had arrived outside his door.

Suddenly Izzy said, Snap! Then he said, snap snap snap. You thought how when you repeat a word over and over, after a while it doesn't make sense any more. Snap snap. This pack isn't all there, he said, careless girl, her mind was always on other things. Do you like fireworks, Lily? Yes, Mr Mordecai. *She* liked fireworks. Things that made her heart go thump. I've got a full pack somewhere, Izzy said, and stood up, As he stood, the lace curtain fell down to join his longjohns on the floor.

You didn't want to look. You didn't want to be there. You didn't know embarrassment could be like this, so extreme, like a white fire. You thought it was the most terrible moment of your life. Izzy looked down at himself, then up at you and began to wail. He took a step towards you with his arms open, and tripped over his longjohns. Swish bang swish.

ISLA! you screamed. ISLA!

The poor wee man, she said. Be a pet now Lily, run across the road and dial 999.

That was the day Izzy went into hospital and everyone stopped locking their doors. You experimented with leaving yours ajar, first a little, then a lot. It felt nice. You were glad he'd gone, but still the big house was like a tooth with a hole in it. His rooms drew you to them. You ended up hanging over the banisters halfway up the stairs, undecided. You thought you should look for the plastic bag, but if you rummaged through his things when he hadn't said you could, he would know. His things would be watching you.

Isla went to visit Izzy the next day, speeding off down the long street and disappearing at the end of it. You hung around by the front door, playing up and down the steps, waiting for Izzy to emerge from the vanishing point slow as a walking crow. In your

Stef Pixner

game two sisters lived at the bottom of the stairs and two brothers at the top and you took turns at playing all the different parts. When Isla got back she told you that Izzy had got very bad. Moses was at his bedside waving a piece of paper in front of him to sign. Izzy had been too weak to refuse.

The day after, when Isla came back from the hospital, Izzy was dead.

You knew you'd got to do it now. Luckily both Isla and your mother had shopping to do. As soon as they'd gone out, you opened the door to the big rooms Izzy had long ago shared with his sister. Everything should have looked different now he was dead. There should have been a bluish light coming off everything, or a greenish one. There should have been music like the music in a thriller. But it was all the same as before. Izzy's Bible on the kitchen table open at the story of God's betrayal of Esau under a piece of toast. The bear, the bicycles, the prams, the smell. You held your nose.

The trouble was, looking for Izzy's money, there were a lot of plastic bags. You remembered the kind Izzy had put the money in, but you couldn't see any like that. It might be under one of the other bags. Or in a different one. Or not in a bag at all any more, but somewhere else. Or in lots of places. And what would you do if you found it, anyway? Give it to your Mum and Dad? Or Isla? You'd have to. But they'd hand it over to Moses, after all, because of the law. You wanted it. You wanted to buy a horse. It could live in the garden. The students wouldn't mind.

You heard the front door go but it wasn't your mother or Isla coming home from the shops. It was Moses letting himself in with Izzy's key, striding down the hallway and bursting ruddy-faced into the room. What are you doing? He said in a shocked angry way. You've got no business in here. Hold your hands out in front of you. You held them out and they trembled with your secret. Once he'd checked they were empty, he behaved like you weren't there. First he made a beeline for the bookshelves. He took every book off every shelf one at a time and shook each one but nothing fell out except bus tickets and insects' wings. He dropped the books onto the floor in a heap, bending back their pages and breaking their spines. Then he took a knife from Izzy's

Hah!

kitchen drawer and slashed the bear from neck to crotch and pulled its kapok insides out. After that he felt around the cracks and crevices of the big bouncy prams. When he didn't find anything there, be emptied out the tea caddy and the sugar tin. He'd brought with him a crowbar to lever up the floorboards, but the floor had so many plastic bags strewn over it, he started on them instead.

The first was full of dirty socks. The next rattled with milk bottle tops. A third had potato peelings in it and was crawling with maggots. It stunk so bad you took a few steps back and bumped into the kitchen table, which reminded you, and you said to Moses, can I have Izzy's Bible? And pointed. You thought just *maybe*. First Moses held it up and shook it. He looked for pages stuck together and special compartments hollowed out of them, flicking the pages like a bank clerk. Then he brought it over. You thought Izzy might have left you a clue written down somewhere in the margins of Genesis chapters 25 to 28, but instead he had scribbled, *No!* and *Call this justice? Good!* and *Oh yes?* and *Hah!* which didn't help. So you went from Esau to Moses who had a lot more words in the book. But though Izzy had written all over the margins of Exodus and Deuteronomy, none of it explained where the money was, unless things like, *Moses saw God in a burning bush, Hah!* or *Moses believes in the state of Israel. I am Israel, and I don't believe!*, were in code.

You watched to see if Moses went back to the plastic bags, you thought you could see a black and white striped one with red writing sticking out from under a pile of others, but the maggots must have put him off because he started rummaging in a chest of drawers instead, throwing things out of each drawer as he went along so they landed on top of the broken books, socks, sugar, tea and milkbottle tops.

Just then the front doorbell went and the knocker, too, and Moses said don't answer it, but you said I've got to Mr Milion, and it was the council who said they'd come to fumigate the ground floor premises. Moses said into your ear, I wasn't doing anything wrong, I'm the next of kin after all. Then the council workers put their masks on and shut the door in both your faces.

At the funeral Izzy was under a black velvet cloth with a Star

Stef Pixner

of David embroidered on it in gold thread on a cart with wheels. You stared at the velvet and found it comforting. You hoped Izzy knew he had a nice cover on him. Moses sat in the front row because he was family. Isla sat in the row after that because she'd known Izzy thirty years. You sat in the back row on your own looking at all the empty chairs. The rabbi sang the Kaddish and the beautiful sounds rolled around the four of you like a starry sky. Isla crossed herself, although you knew she wasn't a Catholic. The rabbi said every life was of equal importance to God. From under the black cloth you heard Izzy say, Hah!

On the way home on the bus Isla said will you come in for a wee cup a tea when we get back? The two of you sat either side of the gas fire which being August wasn't on with Laddy in between and she burned a fag. She said Izzy never spoke to his sister again after Dolly married Moses. Not for twenty years. Not even when Dolly was dying. Then just as you were walking out of the kitchen after three cups of tea Isla said here, Izzy wanted you to have this, and she handed you a bag. It had a knot in it and a note on a gas bill envelope pinned to to the striped plastic with the words, *TO DOLLY, ALL I HAVE*. You ran down the stairs and then towards Becky's with the bag in your hand, shouting, I'm going to get a horse! I'm going to get a horse! A horse called Dolly! And off you ran, down the long street, under the speckled trees, towards the vanishing point.

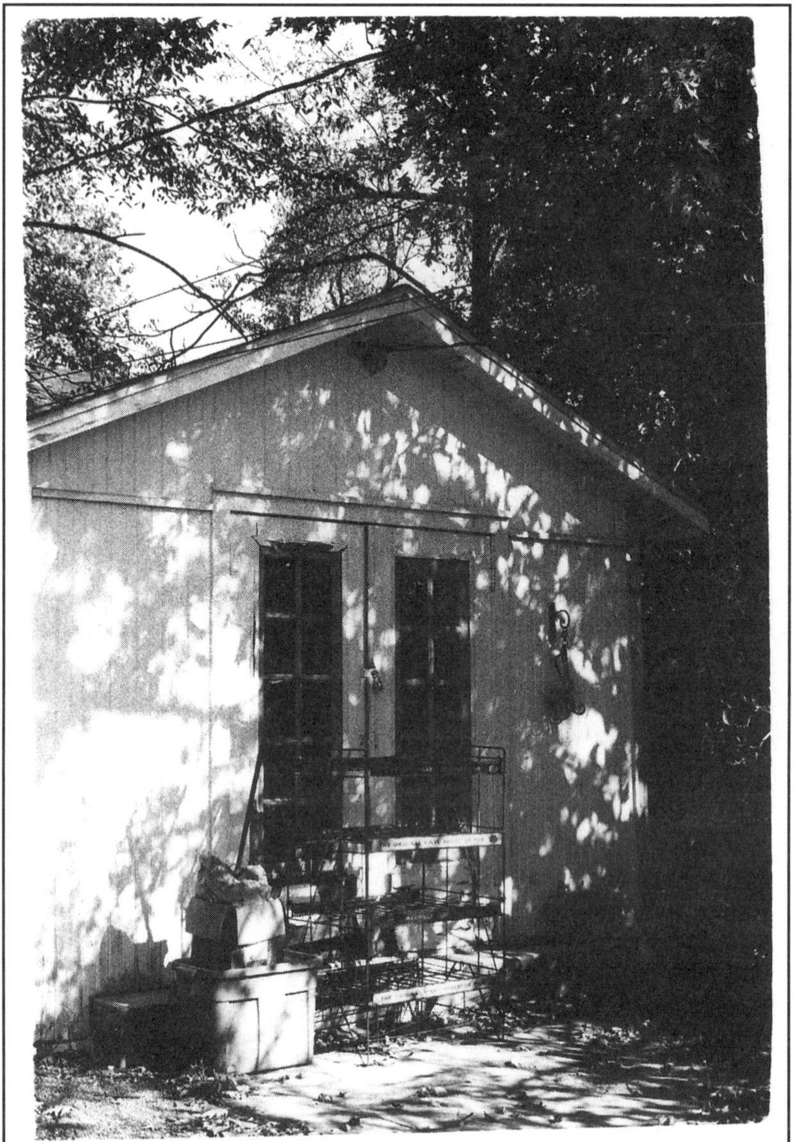

> *George Szirtes*
> **The Late Flight
> of Georges Braque**
> For *George Maclennan*

1. A FABLE

I want to think of it in terms of a fable, a fable about an artist and a bird. The artist is Georges Braque, renowned as a pioneer of the school of painting referred to as Cubism. Braque concentrates his efforts on one essential subject: the clutter of his studio. This studio contains the usual objects: tables, bottles, chairs, a few vases, a stove, a bust or two, an easel, musical instruments, even the occasional life model. Cubism entails an analysis of the space and forms before the artist in terms of geometrical solids – a whole lot of straight lines and angles in other words, though, for the sake of variety if nothing else, it is nice to balance this with a few well chosen curves. Where do these curves come from? Well, vases for instance, or guitars, or busts, or possibly the life model. Since our artist's temperament appears to be sober and classical it is no surprise that the curves should approximate to abstracted forms. The sensuality is in the balance only. It is all *luxe* and *calme*, but rather less than *volupté*. Nevertheless the curve is crucial. There are always fewer curves than straight lines but we know how to read them: these are vases, busts, guitars, palettes, bodies et cetera; those are chairs, tables, easels, books, windows and so forth.

We can read these shapes most of the time because we have learned to read them. Our readings have, of course, a history and history breeds expectations: we expect to find things and therefore we do. They don't look that much like tables, bottles and chairs, but that's what they are. We recognise the shapes as objects, partly

The Late Flight of Georges Braque

because we have learned Braque's language. We read his colours too: earth colours for the most part, the colours of Attic vases, the colours of restraint. We read into them a self-contained world of forms and associations: a world at peace with itself.

At some point the Braque of our fable grows a little bored of the clutter of his studio. Some other curved shape is required. This roundness here, he says, instead of making it into a guitar, could become a bird's breast, and the neck of the guitar, given a little more suppleness in the line, could be turned into the bird's neck. Birds and guitars, in the purely formal sense, have certain things in common. Soon he has made a bird: a most unlikely bird flying through his studio. It remains a classical-cubist kind of bird, but it does introduce a certain dynamic element into the still lives surrounding it. It is, after all, in flight. Naturally, this is disruptive: firstly because it is a moving object among non-moving ones (diagonal lines and scissor-like incisions were all the suggestions of movement allowed in the studio), secondly because a bird in a studio is unusual. It is an object requiring explanation and interpretation. So interpretation begins, not necessarily as a methodical enquiry, but a curiosity, a hunch, one step followed by another. One flap of the wings after another. The interpretation is a poetic process.

Where is this bird leading him? What kind of symbol, what sort of change does it represent? The next time he paints the bird, possibly out of sheer curiosity, Braque introduces elements of realism. This bird is far more literal. Far more your ordinary punter's idea of a bird. But not quite. Not exactly. Texture. The texture of feathers. This is now a bird with weight, a heavy bosomy thing, flapping laboriously through the static, classical, late cubist studio. Its substance, both physically and metaphorically, is elsewhere: it now requires its own physical space and a different level of interpretation. It has irrupted into the ordered world of the studio, a metaphysical studio by now, and is working its mischief reordering space.

The Braque of my fable is old by now. He feels his energy flying from him. Perhaps he might even have begun to consider that energy as his soul, but that's not really the point. The point is that this bird he has invented, and yet not quite invented, for it only arrived following a period of evolution (he first drew it back in 1929, as an illustration to Hesiod) cannot stay in the studio for ever. It is in the wrong space. The bird is being summoned off-stage or is summoning itself off-stage, according to some spatial necessity that is all the time opening onto another, non-cubist reality, which, after a lifetime of restraint, begins to seem quite attractive. Birds in this reality, in the reality this notion of space offers, invite a new level of speculation: it is as if the bird were no longer a function of a particular conception of form and space but was being taken almost literally. This bird can no longer revert quite so readily to vase or guitar. It has feathers, not just an outline. The bird begins to appear in a series of its own, in a space that is neither quite inside or outside. It alone fascinates him now, and so he goes on to paint it in its own space, in the sky or seeking its nest. There is nothing left for Braque but to follow his creation. And so, for almost the first time in a long career, he finds himself outside. Pictures of the studio give way to pictures of field and shore. Suddenly he wants to be someone else altogether. Van Gogh for example. The birds gathering above the dark shore remind him of Van Gogh's crows in the cornfield. His last pictures show birds on the shore. At that point the artist, like Van Gogh, dies. End of fable.

Why am I excited and moved by this somewhat crude and fanciful – but only partly fanciful – narrative? The proposition is not entirely clear, I can see that, though, according to the fable, the progress is straightforward enough. The artist establishes a language with its own lexicon. After a while he desires more, and eventually a new language emerges as the function of a theme. The theme itself arrives as if by stealth, and establishes its own linguistic space. This theme proves transformative. The abstract motif becomes a symbol which, ultimately, turns into a reality. The progress of the fable is from art to life. It's at the point that the bird flies through the window that I feel most exhilarated. In that sense it is a fable about freedom. In another it is about something rather uncanny that can be summed up in the old proverb: you paint the devil on the wall and it appears.

We look at a trapezium and see a tabletop. We look at a circle and

The Late Flight of Georges Braque

see a face. Given other circumstances we could see an orange, a breast or the sun or the full moon. But something happens to us when we see any of these things. We take our seeing seriously and we want it to relate to our condition, whatever that is. In a world of straight lines we want a few curves. Let that be a woman's back, or the full belly of a guitar with its full-bellied sound. Suddenly, there it is. Somewhere. Is it the idea of a guitar, the icon of a guitar, the history of the painted guitar? In his first Jordan poem George Herbert asks: 'May no lines pass, except they do their duty / Not to a true, but painted chair?' To him it's a serious, even vital matter. To us it may be no more than a game, but a game we play for serious, knowing it is only a curved line and not a woman's back. Knowing this is what makes us sophisticated, which is not to say the image has lost its power. And say we move from circles to guitars to backs to birds and that this bird corresponds to some desire. What did the archaic torso of Apollo famously say to Rilke in Paris, in the early summer of 1908? *Du musst dein Leben ändern.* 'You must change your life.' And eventually you do. You open the window, climb out and find yourself on a beach looking at a flock of birds which might well be crows, though when you put them down in the painting they are more suggestive marks than descriptions. But we know how to read them. We have no real difficulty with that.

2. TRANSLATION GAMES

There are languages and languages. There are great, territory-covering, vastly-dispersed families of languages and there are the weird, delightful poky corners of patois, pidgin and idiolect. The languages of painting and poetry are different and the relationship between them has long fascinated people. The Greeks used the term *ekphrasis* to mean 'talking about one art in terms of another' and considered it a useful rhetorical exercise to produce 'a vivid description intended to bring the subject before the mind's eye of the listener'. The underlying project is sometimes deemed to be that the description should be the picture, the picture the story, and so forth. THIS becomes, *tout court*, THAT. Theorists divide attitudes to the possibilities of such kind of ekphrasis into three: ekphrastic indifference (it simply can't be done, so what!); ekphrastic hope (imagination and metaphor may compensate or console us for the impossibility of the task); and ekphrastic fear (we may create convincing images, say from literature, but these images may be wrong, or at least disappointing, as in the-film-of-the-book).

There is considerable academic interest in ekphrasis now. Not because anyone thinks the ekphrastic project is realisable in terms of substitution. A description of a painting will never be the painting and a visualisation of a poem cannot be the poem. There are even certain theorists who, taking a dodgy branch-line from Lessing's *Laokoon*, believe that the very attempt to respond to one art form in terms of another is a prototype of gender-oppression and colonialism. The hard aggressive imperial male of the poet's imagination rapes the colonially-oppressed female Other of the painting. Or vice versa. The painting rapes the poem. Keep your hands off her, you swine, whichever the swine, whichever the her is. Interest, nevertheless, exists because poetry and painting, those so-called sister arts, which were at least soul-mates in Braque's time, and particularly in Braque's circle, seem to be enduring a separation. Both speak of experience but say little or nothing about it to each other. Perhaps they are marooned on other islands, other continents, other heads or parts of the head, driven there by their own incompatible imperatives or banished by external forces. The practical question in ekphrasis now is not so much whether one art can be replaced by another and mean the same thing, but whether there can be useful communication between them at all.

The oppression / colonialization issue surfaces at all levels, and it is no surprise that the issue of translation from one literary text to another should provide another fertile site for theoretical anxiety. I am only a practical poet-cum-translator myself, if you'll excuse the mock-modesty, but the noise of the Seminar Wars occasionally rumbles through the walls of even my cardboard-thin ivory-tower. As with the painting-poetry debate there is not only the issue of how translation should be done, but whether it should be done at all. For the most part I ignore the Seminar

The Late Flight of Georges Braque

Wars because other noises seem more urgent. There is, for example, the voice of the writer-who-might-be-translated who, most of the time, very much wants to be translated ('She was asking for it, m'lud'), especially if the language into which he or she is locked is as obscure as Hungarian. I feel a certain obligation to her, and I am going to call that writer *her* as at least half of the time, in my case, it is indeed a woman. Then there are the voices of the cultural field she represents, who see themselves as being represented through her. Then there are those other voices who justly remind my English-language readers that insularity is not only stifling, but smacks rather more of imperial exclusion than translation does, even when, as occasionally happens, the translated text becomes the literary equivalent of chicken tikka masala. Better that than pig ignorance, they cry. At least you've come so far. Meanwhile, the Seminar Wars continue to be fought, and every so often there are not only bulletins from the front, but certain changes in the very landscape to indicate that this or that territory is henceforth mined (or liberated, but you know how war talk employs its chosen terms).

Translation is a complex act and encompasses a range of activities, among which is the kind of semi-conscious exegesis involved in the reading of any text in its original language by a native speaker of that language. It depends who is reading, where, when, under what circumstances, and though there is inevitably argument about what common ground might be staked out, once it has been decided whether the poem is more to do with chickens than with eggs, or indeed with central heating systems, there is room for productive disagreement. We may also agree, following the line taken by Walter Benjamin, that the true poem is in some sense 'under' this or that language, that it refers to an ur-language that the actual language shadows, and that perhaps, in some Orphean kind of manner, we may be able to get in touch with the poem under the poem, the picture under the picture, the music under the music, the reality under its façade and its interpretations. And there are moments when we feel that we, instinctively but perfectly 'really', understand the poem, or picture; that it speaks to us, as depth speaking to depth. It's a dizzying sensation. Indeed it is the very moment when an intense

George Szirtes

ekphrastic fear may properly begin to set in, but what are you to do? You continue writing or reading the poem, writing or reading the translation, painting or responding to the picture or watching the film-of-the-book, realising that there is inevitably a faint taste of chicken tikka masala in the experience, but that that is to be allowed for, that the work you are facing is more than the sum of its parts and agendas, including your own, including even this one. You trust your feeling that Keats is probably a great poet, and that the theorist of ekphrasis, W.J.T. Mitchell, who accuses Keats of putting banalities ('Beauty is Truth, Truth Beauty...') in the mouth of his Grecian Urn, may be missing something worth having.

3. BRAQUE AND THE POETS

It was at the exhibition at the Royal Academy in 1997, of late works by Georges Braque, that his treatment of the bird in the studio began to intrigue me. The bulk of the work displayed was dominated by the three major late themes of his life: *The Billiard Table* (1944-1952), The *Studio* or *Atelier* series, (1949-1956) and *The Bird* paintings, that take him through to his death in 1963. From the mid-fifties onwards he was painting outdoor landscapes and seascapes too, near his house in Varengeville. The facts, when you check them, aren't quite as in my fable. Apart from a period of some seventeen years between 1911 and 1928, Braque did execute a number of landscapes throughout his career, though those were not on show at the RA, whereas the last pieces were. Nor is the fable absolutely accurate in regard of the development of the bird. His birds don't exactly put on feathers, though they do become more textured. At one point, in the *Atelier VI* of 1950-51, the flying bird stops to perch on an easel before flying off again. You don't, I hope, in all fairness, expect fables to be documentaries with regard to chronologies, and there is in fact no firm consensus as to when each picture in the series was completed, since Braque was in the habit of working on several pictures at once. So while we know that *Atelier IX* (1952-1956), in which the bird seems almost to explode out of its jagged earth-coloured ground, was painted after *Atelier VI*, we would still find it difficult to trace a

The Late Flight of Georges Braque

single line of thought through them, if only because another large studio picture, *The Echo* (1953-1956) was being painted at the same time and here the bird is distinctly feathered, though probably dead. And as for a window for the bird to fly through, there are few windows, if any, in the *Atelier* series.

Nevertheless, the next time we see the bird it is outside: *The Fire-Bird* of 1954 is speeding over a river. The following year Braque paints *The Bird Returning to Its Nest* (a very large work). Then the birds appear as large black shapes against a plain densely-painted sky (*The Black Birds*, 1956-7). There is also a curious vertical picture called *Composition with Stars* (1954-8) in which both stars and bird appear in the studio. And so the bird theme continues, as if Braque were grappling with the idea, unsure whether to stay in or go out. It's too late really: the birds are mostly outside now.

I don't intend reading these birds in themselves. The bird may be supposed to stand for the soul or for peace or for desire or anything else but it would not help me to identify and isolate any one option. Braque himself denied that the birds had any symbolic meaning. Everything, he said, 'is subject to metamorphosis, everything changes according to the circumstance. So, when you ask me whether a particular form in one of my paintings depicts a woman's head, a fish, a vase, or a bird, or all four at once, I can't give you a categorical answer, for the "metamorphic" confusion is fundamental to what I am out to express.' The ambiguity is inbuilt. Not that the word of the artist or the poet is necessarily the last word on this or any other matter regarding interpretation, but poets and artists may at least be presumed to recognise their own processes from a relatively privileged position. Poetry, in both its making and its reading, feeds on ambiguity and poets adored Braque. Reverdy, Ponge, Paulhan, René Char, Saint-John Perse and Apollinaire were all drawn to him at different times. They had no desire to fix the meaning of Braque's work any more than they wanted their own meanings fixed. The poetic project was not to replace his pictures with words but to allow his pictures to generate poems; to allow the language of the pictures to awaken new language in the poems. It was two-way traffic, they felt. The essay by Sophie Bowness in the RA catalogue reminds us that

George Szirtes

Reverdy regarded Cubism as *poésie plastique* 'because of the powerful influence of poetry on it.' Braque, in his turn, talked about 'the painter's poetics'.

The fact that there are a considerable number of poems about Braque's work suggests that his work offered the poets an appropriate kind of non-binding, not-wholly-defined creative space. The notion of free translation might offer a working analogy. The poem would not exist without the picture: the free translation would not exist without the original text. Beyond the free translation lie further processes of ever greater independence from the original object: the process of influence, the process of building a more general matrix of ideas composed of this and that influence, and so forth. What begins as looking or listening, slowly moves to the condition of dialogue, and eventually becomes a new object. The bird in the studio is a creature in motion, not so much an object, according to Braque, as the embodiment of a metamorphosis, or dialogue, which eventually becomes a new object that, in the bird's case, can actually act on life, if by life we understand what actually happens. Braque's pictorial language changes as a result of its appearance. That is the point of the fable. It is also a model for poetic writing about art, or for art related to literary writing. It is not a model that is always followed. The two models of *ekphrasis*, replacement and generation, are confused, and what sets out to be the latter is too often the former. What, to me, is deeply moving about the fable, is the trajectory of the flight and the quietness and order of Braque's studio before that flight.

'Art and life are one,' said Braque in the Cahiers, translating one experience into the other, and you can see how that might work, how the whole act of reading and translation might work, given a little ambiguity and obscurity in the demanding yet generous spaces of the studio. The poetry is at its most potent in the exhilaration of the bird, after several transformations, as it flies through the window toward its nest, towards autonomous objecthood and life. And Braque following: the living embodiment of ekphrastic hope.

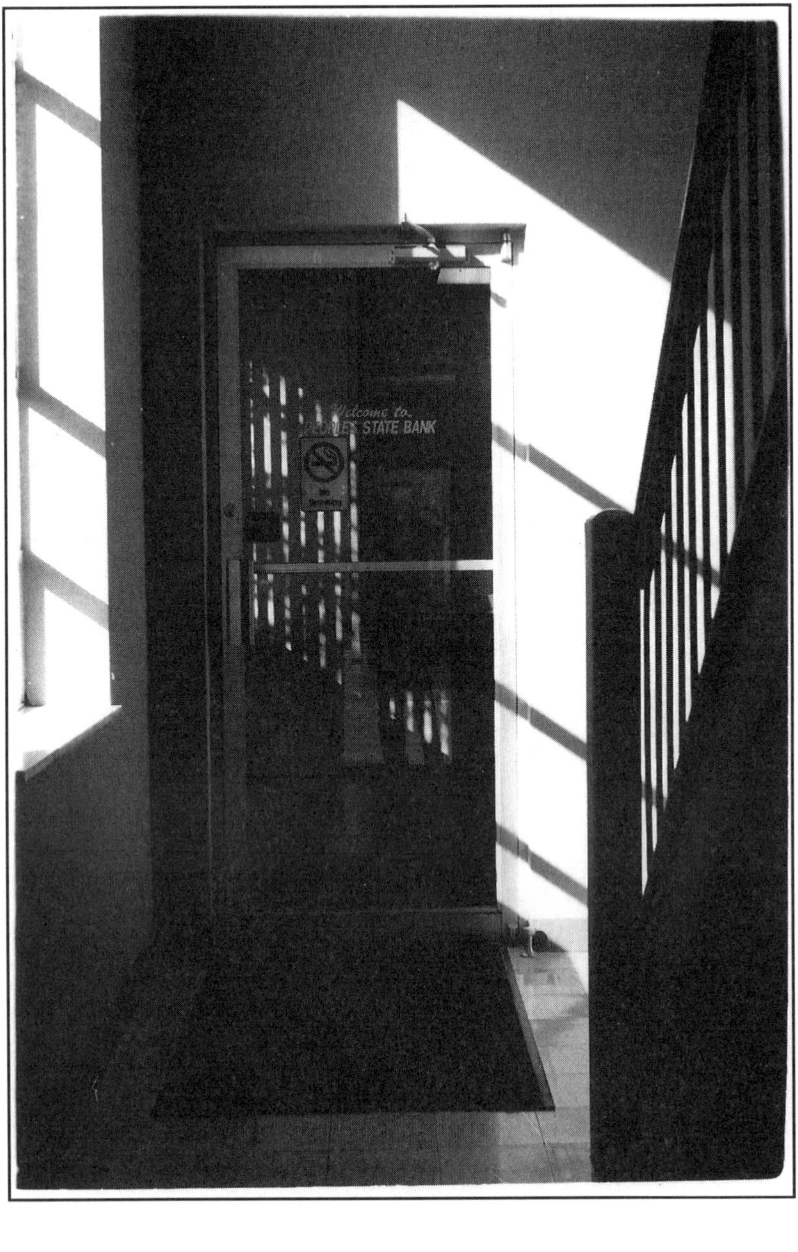
Welcome to
STATE BANK

Thomas Brussig
Am kürzeren Ende der Sonnenallee
(On the Short End of Sunnyside Lane)
An extract translated by *Anne Green*

THE CONDEMNED

They always met at the abandoned playground. They had played there as kids, but no one went there to play any more. No self-respecting fifteen year-old could say he was going to a playground, so they said they were 'hanging at the grounds,' because it sounded more subversive. They'd listen to music there, especially the illegal stuff. Most of the time Mike brought the songs. Right after he taped them from the radio, he'd bring them to the grounds. Many of the songs they listened to were too new to be illegal. It wasn't until a song was outlawed that it became truly popular – like 'Hiroshima' or 'Je t'aime' or every song the Rolling Stones ever did. No one knew who made the songs illegal, much less why. But, at the time, the illegalest of the illegal was 'Moscow, Moscow' from 'Wonderland.'

You were supposed to listen to 'Moscow, Moscow' in a sort of true blues ecstasy – rocking back and forth, with your eyes shut tight and your teeth dug into your lower lip. The point was to get into the blues until there was nothing but the music and your movement. That's why they didn't notice the street cop standing right behind them until it was too late. Just as Mike's friend Mario cried out, 'Oh, man, is this *illegal*. Totally *illegal*,' the cop snapped off the tape recorder and asked, 'What's illegal?'

Mario tried to play dumb. 'Illegal? What do you mean, illegal? Did somebody here say illegal?' But it was quickly apparent that his act wouldn't cut it.

The Condemned

'Oh, you mean *illegal*,' Mike said, feigning relief. 'That's just slang.'

'You see, in the slang of young people, the term "illegal" is used to express their enthusiasm,' explained Four-Eyes, who had read so much he had not only ruined his eyes, but also could spout out arrogant sentences at the drop of a hat. 'According to the youth of today, *illegal* is a word that expresses approval and agreement.'

'Like "nifty" or "neat,"' added Afro. He was called Afro because he had hair like Jimi Hendrix.

Four-Eyes continued his explanation. 'Also popular in the youth culture are the expressions "wild" and "crazy."'

'And those mean the same as "heavy", "horny", "hairy" and, well, "*illegal*,"' explained Blimpy. Everyone nodded enthusiastically and waited for the cop to respond.

'You guys must think I'm stupid.' he said. 'I bet you were talking about how illegal it is not to turn in the passport lost by a woman from the FRG.'

'No,' Mike said, 'I mean yes – of course we know it's totally illegal not to turn in a passport you find. But we weren't talking about that, officer.'

'Sergeant!' corrected the street cop firmly. 'I'm a Sergeant, not an officer. Sergeant is a non-commissioned rank. First you're a Private, then a Corporal, then a Sergeant. Next week I'm being promoted to Second Lieutenant – *that's* an officer's rank.'

'That's great! Congratulations!' Mike enthused, relieved that the street cop had forgotten why he had originally come to the grounds. Instead of investigating the illegal music, he was reciting ranks.

'After Second Lieutenant comes First Lieutenant, Captain, Major, Colonel – all officers' ranks. Then the Generals' ranks: Major General, Lieutenant General, and Four Star General. Do you notice anything about these?'

'That's a lot of ranks,' Afro said. 'And yours seems to be near the bottom of the barrel.'

'He means the best years of your career are still ahead of you,' exclaimed Blimpy, still intimidated and trying to avoid any possible offence.

'No, no, that's not it. If you had paid attention, you'd have noticed that in the officers' ranks the Lieutenant is under the Major, but in the Generals' ranks, the Lieutenant General is above the Major General.'

'How is that possible?' asked Mario.

'The first will be last and the last will be first,' said Four-Eyes. 'That's from the . . .' He wasn't able to finish before Mike elbowed him in the side.

'Next week I'll be a Second Lieutenant and then things will be different around here,' said the street cop. 'If one of you finds a passport from a West German woman, you turn it in to me right away, is that clear?'

'What's her name, this West German woman'?' inquired Four-Eyes, curious as always.

'You should turn in every passport you find. But the passport in question belongs to one Helene Rumpel. What's the woman's name?'

'Helene Rumpel,' recited Mario. Mario was considered the most rebellious in the group because he had the longest hair. Since Mario had given the cop the correct answer, the cop could leave thinking he had asserted his authority.

'Right, Rumpel. Helene Rumpel,' the cop repeated to nods all around. The cop turned to leave, but then changed his mind.

'What was that song you were playing?' He asked slowly. When he received no response, he pressed the play button on the cassette recorder and 'Moscow, Moscow' filled the air. Mike almost shit his pants. The illegalest of all illegal songs. The cop listened intently and finally nodded as if he understood.

'Whose tape is this?' Everyone froze. 'Well, whose cassette is it?'

'Actually, it's mine,' Mike admitted.

'Aha. This, I'm taking with me. I like to listen to music, especially when I'm at the office.' Mike closed his eyes in horror as he imagined 'Moscow, Moscow' being played to a roomful of cops. He heard the Sergeant walk away saying, 'You wouldn't have thought that about me, I'll bet.'

A week later, Mike discovered the cop had not, in fact, been promoted to Second Lieutenant, but had instead been demoted to Corporal. Not surprisingly, the cop started to harass Mike.

The Condemned

Whenever Mike ran into him, the cop would say, 'My name is *Corporal* Horkefeld and I am conducting a search for wanted persons. Identification papers please.'

The first time it happened, Mike took the words 'wanted persons' very seriously, assuming that anyone who listened to 'Moscow, Moscow' sooner or later found himself on the most-wanted list. Later, he put two and two together. It appeared the Sergeant had, as promised, played 'Moscow, Moscow' for his fellow cops. Apparently he had done so at the annual policemen's ball, which was also the time for announcing and celebrating promotions. And because 'Moscow, Moscow' was so very illegal, there must have been a huge scandal. Mike could picture the scene: the chief of police storming to the front of the room, smashing the speakers with his night stick; the Major General drawing his side arm and blasting the tape recorder to bits. Both of them would then have ripped the new lieutenant stripes from Horkefeld's shoulders. It must have been something along those lines – if not worse – to warrant the amount of torment the now lowly corporal inflicted on Mike.

You see, if the cop hadn't taken the 'Moscow, Moscow' cassette, Mike's first love letter wouldn't have ended up in the no-man's land surrounding the Berlin Wall. It's a long story and not an easy one to explain, and although Mike couldn't be sure the letter was for him, or even if it was from the girl of his dreams, it was certainly connected to Sergeant-to-Corporal Horkefeld and his illegal song.

The girl's name was Miriam and she was in the same grade as Mike, but in a different section. She was by far the most beautiful girl in the school – for Mike, she was the most beautiful girl in the world. She was *the* celebrity of Sunnyside Lane. Whenever she came out on the street, a whole new rhythm started. The street workers dropped their jackhammers, the cars stopped to let Miriam cross the street, the soldiers in the watch towers trained their binoculars on her, and the West German school kids' laughter was replaced by a collective gasp.

Miriam had not gone to their school for very long and no one knew much of anything about her. She was exotic, beautiful, mysterious, and, as the result of a wrong turn, Miriam was,

Thomas Brussig

strictly speaking, an illegitimate child. While on his way to the Justice of the Peace to marry Miriam's mother, then in her eighth month of pregnancy, Miriam's father made a wrong turn and found himself hopelessly lost. Miriam's father, who was from Dessau, didn't know East Berlin at all. So when he found his progress blocked by the security checkpoint on Sunnyside Lane, he didn't understand that it was a border crossing into West Berlin and cursed and yelled and pounded on the horn of his Trabant. 'I want to get through!' he screamed.

Cars got lost in East Berlin all the time and often ended up at checkpoint crossings. Most drivers were simply given directions and sent on their merry way. But Miriam's enraged father caused such a commotion that the border guards decided to take him more seriously. He was questioned for so long that he missed his own wedding. And before the next appointment with the judge arrived, Miriam was born; thus entering the world as an illegitimate child.

After her little brother was born, Miriam knew her parents would split up. Her father had gone a bit insane. Frequently locking himself out of the apartment, he would either kick the front door in or start screaming like a banshee, embarrassing the family in front of the entire neighborhood. When her parents finally divorced, Miriam's mother naturally wanted to get as far away from her crazy husband as possible, so she moved to the short end of Sunnyside Lane. She knew that Miriam's father would always and forever avoid that street.

Miriam's relationships with the opposite sex were difficult to understand. Four-Eyes said that Miriam acted like a typical child of divorce – secretive, aimless, disillusioned. She was often seen climbing on the back of a motorcycle that pulled up to her door just as she dashed out of her house. The motorcycle was an AWO – an extremely rare machine. It was the only four-cylinder motorcycle in the entire east block: they had stopped building them in the early 1960s. None of the guys in Mike's group had a moped, much less a motorcycle. Afro was the only one who even had a bicycle. And if any of them had owned a motorcycle, it would have been one of those noisy two-cylinder junkers. Simply by climbing on the back of an AWO, it was clear to all the guys

The Condemned

at the grounds that Miriam moved in a completely different world.

Whenever Miriam heard that intoxicating four-cylinder rumble, she ran out, kissed the driver quickly, and was gone. No one ever saw the guy's face.

'Maybe he's not her boyfriend,' Mike said one day. 'Maybe he's just . . .' But no matter how hard he tried, he couldn't think of anyone who could pick up the prettiest girl in the world, get a kiss, and not be her boyfriend.

'Maybe he's her uncle,' Mario said scornfully. He was also in love with Miriam, but he didn't romanticize her like Mike did. Once, he asked Mike, 'Do you want to go out with her, or do you want to worship her?' 'First, I want to worship her,' Mike answered with all sincerity.

'Okay, then what?'

'Then I want to die for her.'

Mike recognized that he was obviously not ready to go out with any girl, if he only wanted to worship and then die for her.

Mike couldn't even bring himself to talk to Miriam – even when given a perfect opportunity, like when she was in front of him in the cafeteria line. He always fell apart.

Mike did try to find out about Miriam though, through her little brother. Everyone who had a crush on Miriam – and that was all the boys in the high school – tried to get information about Miriam from her little brother. Miriam's little brother was only ten, but he knew what his info was worth. He took bribes in the form of Matchbox cars. Whenever anyone wanted to know something about Miriam, he'd ask, 'Got any Matchies?' Soon, all the older boys became experts on Matchbox cars. Their relatives in the West were surprised that fifteen and sixteen year-olds asked for a Matchbox Lamborghini or Corvette for Christmas. Miriam's little brother didn't take just any old car. One time Four-Eyes tried to give him a boring green truck, but Miriam's little brother brushed him off. He wanted a Maserati or a Jaguar – and it had to be in perfect condition.

Miriam's little brother enjoyed other privileges as well. No one could touch him. When one of his classmates threatened to beat him up, he knew the older boys would save him. And the older

Thomas Brussig

boys didn't touch him either, regardless of how much he taunted them. Miriam's brother was as untouchable as Miriam herself.

Once, when push came to shove, Mike did try to get Miriam's attention.

It happened after Mike had been sentenced to give a lecture at the next meeting of the 'Free German Youth Group.' Mike's friend Mario had made a slight alteration to the banner hanging in the main entrance of the school. 'The Communist Party is the *foreman* of the working class' became 'The Communist Part is the fore*skin* of the working class.'

Someone had finked – there was always a rat when things like this happened. This time was different, though, because Mario had been caught before. This offence would be 'three strikes and you're out.' Mario needed to graduate to get a job as a mechanic, but now, he was looking at a career as a ditch digger. Since it would only be *his* first offence, Mike took the fall for the 'foreskin incident.' Mike had always wanted to be known for such deeds, and this was a classic. Neither Mario nor Mike knew that the slogan came from Lenin, however, and that made it a heinous offence. Whoever insulted Lenin, insulted the party. Whoever insulted the party, insulted the GDR. And whoever insulted the GDR was an enemy of freedom itself. And the enemies of freedom *had to be fought*. And it certainly looked as though Mike had insulted Lenin. Thus, Gertrude Lardenhauser, the school principal, sentenced Mike to give a lecture.

Although it was allegedly an honor, having to give a lecture at a Free German Youth meeting was a bona fide punishment. No one wanted to do it and everyone tried to get out of it. It was a delicate art, coming up with an excuse to avoid speaking for the Free German Youth. You had to sound sincere, as if you really wanted to speak, but, alas, you were unable to due to unfortunate circumstances. 'There are so many students who are better speakers than I am.' 'I can't possibly say anything that would be worthy of such an honor.' 'I don't have time to prepare because my mom is sick.' 'I gave one last year and surely someone else deserves a chance.' Mike couldn't talk himself out of it, though. He had sinned and this was penance. His lecture was entitled, 'What the quotations of Marx and Lenin mean to us today.' Mike

The Condemned

was afraid that if the first thing Miriam ever heard from him was 'The Quotations of Marx and Lenin,' she'd think of him as 'Little Mr Red.' He had to act and act fast.

He had two weeks until the lecture, just a few days after the school dance. The dance was always during the first month of the school year, before anyone could be grounded for bad grades. Since it ended at nine o'clock, the dance never really got going. Even so, Mike thought it was his best bet to get Miriam to notice him.

But of course, the dance turned out to be the absolute worst bet. All the boys came with the same objective as Mike. But Miriam wasn't there. Only after Mike, Mario, Afro, Four-Eyes and Blimpy had peeled the labels off a battalion of pop bottles did Miriam finally make her entrance. She immediately started blabbing with one of her friends like they hadn't seen each other in ten years. Miriam's friend was called 'Shrapnel' behind her back, because some kid had said her face must have been hit by a load of it. Mike knew it would be nearly impossible to find someone to go with him to ask Shrapnel to dance. Even Mario refused. 'I know I owe you Mike, but don't even think of asking me to dance with *her*.'

Mike had to go it alone. So in the break between songs, he began the torturous trek across the dance floor. Just as the first notes of the next song sounded, he asked Miriam, 'Wanna dance?' He tried to appear nonchalant, but quickly realized he was doomed. He had just done the most embarrassing thing in his entire life. The song they were playing was an East-Block number of the worst kind! The worst of the worst – a Czech tune! The dance floor cleared in a flash. Miriam and Shrapnel interrupted their conversation for a fraction of a second, glanced at Mike from the corner of their eyes, before continuing where they left off. The whole room – the whole *school* – was witness to his humiliation. Mike stood there like a statue, but Miriam and Shrapnel went on as if he didn't exist. So he had to slink back across the dance floor with the entire school starring at him. Afro said, 'That's one brave man,' which was what everyone was thinking. Mike was the first who had dared ask Miriam to dance.

Mike sat like a lump in his chair until an elbow from Mario

broke his trance. Something had happened – something big. Four-Eyes had taken off his glasses and was cleaning them nervously. Blimpy stared at the dance floor with his mouth hanging open and said, 'This can't be happening.' But it was. Miriam was dancing – and not with Shrapnel. She was dancing with a *guy*. No one knew who. He had just waltzed in with a few friends, gone directly to Miriam, and asked her to dance. His friends had asked other girls to dance - but only the best looking girls in the place. And they were dancing to a love song. The longest of long, slow love songs. A love song so slow and so long, that if you got a chance to dance with a girl to this song, you never forgot it. From that point on, the world was divided into those who had done it, and those who hadn't. The chosen, enlightened ones, and the poor slobs, cheated out of a cosmic experience.

But Miriam didn't just dance with this mystery boy, she started necking with him. Mike saw them, the other guys saw them – *everybody* saw them. Suddenly, the lights came on and Gertrude Lardenhauser came storming through the room. Loverboy was wearing a T-shirt from John F. Kennedy High School. Miriam had been necking with a West-Berliner! Gertrude Lardenhauser made a huge scene and threw the West-Berliner out. Miriam was immediately sentenced to give a lecture at the next meeting of the 'Free German Youth Group.' Suddenly, Mike was the man of the hour.

In the days that followed, the ninth and tenth grade boys all tried to do something bad enough to have to give a lecture. But the administration had established a two-scapegoat-per-meeting limit. There were always several officers from the FGY who came to these meetings, and they might look poorly on a school that had too many students giving lectures. Even so, many infractions occurred in the days after the dance. In Physics class, when Afro was asked what one should do in the event of an atomic explosion, he answered, 'First, take a good look, because you'll only see it once. Second, lie down and crawl to the nearest cemetery. And third, crawl slowly so you don't cause a panic.' He got an 'F,' not a lecture. In Phys. Ed., Mario threw his hand grenade only four feet. He meant to look like a pacifist, but the teacher made him do fifty push-ups – ten clapping – to build his

The Condemned

strength. He didn't get a lecture either. Blimpy got caught trying to take the flag down from the pole in front of the school. Trying to take the flag down bordered on terrorism, but Blimpy didn't have to give a lecture, either – he only had to carry the flag in the parade honoring the founding of the GDR. This turned out to be an even worse punishment than giving a lecture, because it rained cats and dogs on that day. Everyone put in a brief appearance and disappeared, but Blimpy had to stay on his feet with the huge flag, which grew heavier and heavier in the pouring rain. It got so heavy that it had to be held at an angle so that you could see the emblem. It was all Blimpy could do to make it through the parade holding the soaked flag in front of him.

Mike remained the only one who had to give a lecture. Besides Miriam, of course.

First contact was made in the dark, backstage of the auditorium. Miriam was late, and the meeting had been in full swing for some time. The party official droned on and on with her endless report of the official numbers for that quarter. The party official could put everything into percentages: grades in Russian, enlistments in three, ten, or twenty-five years of military service; charitable giving to other communist countries; membership in the Free German Youth; school field trips; science fairs; library visits, and on and on and on. When the party official began to recite the percentage of participants in the 'milk break' program ('7.4% of students in the ninth grade drink whole milk with 2.8% fat, which is an increase of 2.2% . . .'), the first kids started to snooze. The only one who didn't have to fight off sleep was Mike. But he was waiting backstage.

Then Miriam arrived, not wearing her FGY shirt, giggling and whispering, 'Oh, gosh, I'm late, I'm late. Am I in the right place?' Mike wanted to tell her that she was always in the right place, but was so overwhelmed that he could only nod and whisper, 'Yes, right.' It was dark and cramped backstage. He had never been so close to Miriam before. She looked at Mike for a minute, then turned around and took off her T-shirt. She wasn't wearing anything underneath. 'Don't peek!' she whispered slyly and Mike forgot how to breathe. Miriam pulled her FGY shirt out of a bag and put it on. She hadn't even buttoned all the buttons when she

Thomas Brussig

turned back to Mike. He was paralyzed.

'So,' whispered Miriam. 'What did you do?'

'Huh?' Mike spluttered, unsure what she was asking.

'Well, you must have done something pretty bad to get this gig.'

'Oh, yeah, sure,' Mike said, no longer whispering, but practically shouting, unable to control himself. Anyone in the auditorium could have heard him if they'd been awake. 'I insulted Lenin, and the working class, and the party. I'm sure you know what I did.'

It seemed though, that the more Mike tried to impress Miriam, the more bored she became. 'So, anyway, they caught me and they almost threw me . . .'

'The guys in the West kiss different than we do,' interrupted Miriam in a romantic voice. Mike swallowed and was silent. 'I'd really like to show someone,' she whispered, giggling. Then she stopped giggling, as if an idea had occurred to her. Mike sensed just *which* idea had occurred to her. It was so cramped backstage – Mike couldn't move even if he had wanted to. In the darkness he saw her sensuous lips glistening. She slowly moved closer to him. He knew that her wonderfully full breasts were pressing freely into the fabric of her FGY shirt. He smelled her soft, flowery scent. He shut his eyes and thought, 'No one will ever believe me . . .'

It was at that very moment the party official finished her litany of numbers and called Miriam to the podium. It was dark backstage, but not so dark that Miriam couldn't see the disappointment on Mike's face. 'I'll show you some other time,' she said with a last little giggle, before going to the podium to deliver her lecture. She let it be known that she found those boys who signed up for three years of military service, instead of the usual two, very manly – and that she would, of course, remain true to any man who signed up for three years. Gertrude Lardenhauser nodded in agreement. Only Mike could see from backstage that Miriam had crossed her fingers.

Mike was so intoxicated by this 'near kiss' with Miriam that he deviated from his prepared manuscript after only a few sentences. 'My fellow Free German Youths, I would like to talk to you today

The Condemned

about the importance of knowing the works of the giants in Communist Theory – Marx and Lenin. Their thoughts were permeated by a . . . great . . . undying . . . Love.' When Mike uttered the word 'love,' his eyes began to shine and he was gripped by such euphoria that he lost all control. 'It was a Love that made them invincible. A Love that allowed them to slip like butterflies from the cocoon that had imprisoned them, to fly free and happy through this wonderful world, to fly over beautiful fields full of fragrant and colorful flowers . . .' Blimpy looked at Mario and asked quietly 'Did someone spike his food?' Mario whispered back, 'If they did, I want some too.'

Mike's enthusiasms led Gertrude Lardenhauser to follow his speech with her own question: 'Can a revolutionary be passionate?' in order to answer it with, 'Yes, a revolutionary *can* be passionate!'

Mario had to hold Mike down, otherwise he would have leapt up and yelled, wide-eyed, 'Yes, yes, let's all be passionate!'

After the meeting, Mike went over to Miriam and confessed. 'I saw you cross your fingers.' 'Really?' giggled Miriam. 'Then I guess we have a secret.' Then she ran to the exit, leaving Mike standing there. Mike had heard the unmistakable rumble of a four-cylinder motorcycle as well, but he ran after Miriam anyway, arriving just in time to see her ride off. It didn't matter. 'She promised me a kiss. She promised me a kiss,' he thought joyously the entire way home. No one could spoil his good mood – not even a frustrated beat cop asking for his ID.

Owen Marshall
When Gravity Snaps

We were waiting in the Pathways bus a block from Cologne Cathedral, which was the reason for the tour's morning stop. The stained glass windows were fiery in the dark church, and if I closed my eyes while waiting in the bus, the narrow windows rose in my mind like brilliant, illuminated candles. Other tours in other buses waited beside us in the morning sun, and the busy city swirled past. The couple from Gibraltar were holding us up of course. At scenic or heritage stops the Gibraltar couple were always late; after shopping stops the Wisconsin Foursome were inevitably to blame. Our tour guide, Malcolm, bounced in and out of the bus as his impatience grew. 'Anyone seen the Gambaegges?' But no one replied. Malcolm began a tuneless whistle, and shot his wrist abruptly from his jacket to make a watch check. The departure of our Rhine tour boat was a deadline beyond any negotiation.

All bus groups have their Gambaegges and Wisconsin Foursomes, and they become the scapegoats for everything malign and disappointing that happens. Maybe they weren't directly responsible for the snatching of Irene Hamble's bag in Marseilles, or the bruising fall suffered by amiable old Chester at the Lourdes Grotto, but if they hadn't got the whole party behind schedule and hassled, those things wouldn't have happened. Irene Hamble said she only took her bag because there wasn't time to go back and lock it in the bus.

The Wisconsin Foursome were not vicious or immoral people, just two brothers who had married two sisters, and come through excessive and humdrum wealth to the view that the world existed

When Gravity Snaps

for their personal satisfaction. The itinerary so clearly enunciated by Malcolm meant nothing to them: shopping finished when the Wisconsin Foursome had made all of the considerable purchases they deemed necessary, dinner was served in hotels when the Foursome deigned to arrive for theirs, the bus would not leave until they occupied the seats for which they'd paid. The Wisconsin Foursome were not competitive in their late arrivals and at those stops they termed 'Heritage' – galleries, churches, ruins, monuments – would demand the refuge of the bus after a brief territorial examination of the lavatory arrangements. They would sleep in the seats, each face hidden by a baseball cap, each attired in soft, pastel, unisex clothes, so that gender could only be gauged by size. The six foot ones women, the six foot fours, men. The Gambaegges could be relied on to be late at heritage stops, so the Wisconsin Foursome didn't freak out.

The Foursome were preoccupied with their plumbing, which was the term they used for the whole range of bodily functions. I thought maybe their wealth had been founded on plumbing in a more mechanical sense, but no, brother Delmar told me the family business was in remote-controlled security doors and shutters. 'Sliding, rolling, folding, tilting, pop-up, just the whole thing really. I guess,' said Delmar. 'And dressy – clients want their security to look dressy these days, now that's for sure.'

At breakfast the Wisconsin Foursome would run through their night's plumbing history in voices which rattled the pots in hotel kitchens in Brugge and Berlin. 'You got rid of yesterday's gas, Sissy-Anne?' Roy might holler. 'This continental food is something else, isn't it?'

'I haven't had a satisfactory movement for a week, no word of a lie,' Delmar would boom. I had this idea that Wisconsin must be a very under-populated place with passing acquaintances shouting to each other over great distances. In all the time we spent on tour, my wife could never work out which sister was married to which brother, they were in and out of each others' rooms and lives so readily. Delmar, Roy, Sissy-Anne and Blanche appeared interchangeable to us, but each must have had an individual shining core of being locked away in each substantial body.

In Vienna our hotel was in the suburbs, close to a wooded park and, although the shoppers of the party complained, I was happy there. After two days, and a visit to the Summer Palace, I was convinced Austria was a calm, courteous and well-appointed place, and have continued to promulgate that view. How assuredly trenchant we become about brief impressions, what powerful, if not entirely accurate, shorthand for 'state of the nation' a brief visit offers.

The only downer was that Trevor started to seek out my company in Vienna. He was a single guy, my countryman, and his ambitions for the European tour were all of sexual gratification. I hoped it was common citizenship and not libidinous interest he thought we shared. Trevor's fantasies were depressingly predictable – he told me at the bar in our Vienna hotel that on his flight to Britain the blonde hostess leant over him with a light ale and murmured, 'Follow me to the starboard aft toilet and you can fuck me over Turkey.'

Trevor did manage to lay one of the Pathways tourists – a skinny Dutch girl with better English than his. They copulated behind one of the abutments of the Mount Pilatus lookout, but at lower altitudes thereafter she treated him with disdain.

At my age I should be immune from others' opinions, but I found it unsettling to be in Trevor's company for very long. The assumption of unseemly topics hung over every conversation, and laughter, or confidences, drew the disapproving glances from the women in the bus. My wife told me not to encourage him, and I never accepted his invitations to alternative evening activities, but stuck to those things sanctioned by the brochure – folk-dancing, yodelling, weaving fests.

More vexing to me than Trevor's gonad philosophy was his dangerous combination of logic and ignorance. He maintained that the mountain tops should be the hottest places because they were closest to the sun, and argued that people were progressively taller the further from the equator they lived because they were always stretching plant-like for the light. Almost everything Trevor said cried out for rebuttal but he was set in all his views, and I learnt it was best to let things pass. I didn't want his prejudices and anomalies to take root in my own mind. My wife said it was too early to say for sure about that.

When Gravity Snaps

Greece is a wonderful place, but unbearably hot. I stood in awe at Thermopylae, and was seized with a sense of occasion on the Acropolis, despite the relentless sun and the vigilant whistling custodians who kept us from touching the marble. The heat drove me down to the bus park, where the Wisconsin Foursome lay across double seats with baseball caps for faces, and allowed their plumbing a rumbling ease. Old Chester sat beside me with his wrinkled, sunburnt arms, and answered questions the official guide had glossed over. Chester had been Reader in Classics at London University and was full of esoteric and loving information, if you took the trouble to ask. He was equally happy to watch all in silence, and annotate his observations no doubt within his capacious mind.

A few days later, when we were sailing back to Piraeus from our Greek Island tour, the setting sun caught the Parthenon in a pink, luminous glow. For a moment I was transported nearly two and a half thousand years back, for I saw just what weary Athenians had seen from their homecoming triremes, and the wonder of it overcame the crowded gossip of my fellows at the deck supper tables, and the pounding of a modern engine. The skinny Dutch girl complained about the shipboard wine; Chester's mouth dropped open and he stood in the slump of old age and marvelled at history recaptured in the setting sun. I wanted to join him and share the moment, but Nick Guillermo began talking to me about the exchange rates Malcolm had arranged.

Nick was an Italian-Australian – his parents had emigrated in the late 1950s and made a new life in Melbourne. Nick was born in Australia, or was very young when they went there, and he was on the tour with his widowed mother, mainly so she could return to her home close to Turin and see if she was remembered. If his mother was well received she might not want to go on with the tour, and he was worried they wouldn't get any refund. He wasn't going to say anything about it to Malcolm though, in case it all came to nothing. There was some ambivalence about the family"s status in the village – from the little Nick said about it I thought maybe his grandfather had been a Fascist.

'The assistant engineer told me all the tour guides work a

swiftie with currency transactions,' said Nick. 'Malcolm's ripping us off for sure.' Nick had a lugubrious conviction that all the world was corrupt, while Mrs Guillermo was cheerful, trusting and a favourite on the bus. Nick told me at various times that the Greek waiters were pickpockets, the wine watered-down on the Côte d'Azure, the Swiss had a spy in each hotel, and Russian women trapped you into marriage by sexual provocation. From my own experience I could comment on only one of these accusations – the wine was indeed watered-down in the seaside cafés of Menton. It was a weak rosé, chilled to hide its faults.

'Oh, maybe it's better that way,' cried Mrs Guillermo, who was perhaps practising to placate her Italian relations.

The greatest test of friendship is the good fortune of one of those involved. Gillian Reading and Naomi Browne were mid-career friends in the short-term contract world of regional television. There was a thunderstorm on the night we stayed in Brindisi and the lightning showed the ancient port at its worst, all choppy water and debris. In the morning, as we waited for the ferry, squeezed between the damp land and the falling cloud, Naomi received a cell phone call saying she had been appointed presenter for a twenty-six episode series on Scottish cuisine, and Gillian heard she was out on her ear. No one says the world is fair, but the obvious can be a form of injustice too. Naomi was younger, better looking, had a more outgoing nature and long, pale hands which suited Scottish cooking.

With such differing outcomes both Naomi and Gillian had to carry on the tour, though at a stroke all was changed. Naomi could see everything in the rosy tints of success and anticipation; Gillian must have felt the chill of descent. But how wonderfully she persisted in her friendship and in her openness to new experience. I wanted to congratulate her on her character, but knew of no way of doing so without it sounding like commiseration.

In Barcelona, after the tour to see the Gaudi architecture and some Roman ruins partly exposed, like fat women's thighs, in an underground chamber, I wandered in a broad avenue which went down to the sea. The length of the avenue was crowded with market stalls down its centre, and the mass of people in the warm dusk pushed past each other with accustomed indifference. By a

When Gravity Snaps

trestle table of original and execrable miniature art was a bench occupied by two men and a woman, but there was half a rump of seat exposed and I squeezed on, smiling and nodding to excuse myself. The three Spaniards showed no annoyance. They each gave up a little of their own space; they were accustomed to living in a crowded city. They didn't seen to know each other, and the four of us sat tightly packed amid the noise and surge. I could feel the body warmth of the elderly man next to me. He had a slight smell of dry vegetables, or sacking. He had a stick upright between his legs and rested both hands on top, looking at the faces flowing past with a slight smile, as if acknowledging their energy, their urgency, but savvy to the outcome just the same.

Among all those people it was Trevor whom I had to recognize, propositioning a small, deep-chested woman behind a counter of bags and wallets. Trevor wore his hair in a quiff, like a quail's crest, and had a habit of baring his teeth in a false yawn. Even at a distance it seemed to me she didn't find him attractive in any form of transaction. A whole clutch of bum-bags hung from her stall and the zips swung loosely as if their necks were broken. The woman had a blue scarf of very light material, and it fluttered slightly in a breeze I couldn't feel as she rebuffed Trevor, speaking without looking at him while she continued to arrange her stock.

The man beside me stood up with a sigh. He checked the seat to see if he'd left anything of value, then raised his stick slightly to the three of us left on the bench, and was carried off by the flow. He left just the faintest scent of vegetables and sacking, and a less obscured view of the tourist miniatures at the art stall.

In the hotel, much later, I was woken by the Gambaegges arguing in the next room. They began in English and I caught enough to know he was in a fury at her extravagance, and she enduringly bitter concerning his treatment of their only son, whom she felt had been driven from the family by her husband's jealousy and rigidity. Disparate themes to an outsider, but for the Gambaegges a perfectly connected dialogue, as such things are in the web of marriage. The volume declined with the intensity of their anger until English itself was abandoned, and they were hissing at each other in Spanish, or Italian. Finally there was just

Owen Marshall

the sobbing of Mrs Gambaegge, insistent and with a terrible sadness through the wall, and I fell asleep thinking that wherever we are in our life we find happiness to be elsewhere. In all of the public face of the tour the Gambaegges were never apart, but after Barcelona I could never find any irritation in myself when they inconvenienced the rest of us.

The broken necked bum-bags swaying to Trevor's false seduction, the courteous smell of sacking in a warm crowded evening, Gaudi and the midnight weeping of Gibraltar's Mrs Gambaegge are what I have of Barcelona – a pot pourri quite exclusive and true to me.

Malcolm was a young man from Worcester with slightly bulging blue eyes, and impatience just below the surface of his pleasant nature. He wanted the best for all of us and was convinced he knew what that was. He was knowledgeable and not blasé about the places to which he took us, though most he had visited several times before. He told me he had been saving to attend the University of East Anglia to take a degree in languages and history. He spoke French and Italian well, and some German. When his arrangements were under pressure from the Wisconsin Foursome, the Gambaegges, or Irene Hamble, who constantly wished to use the on-board toilet despite the comfort stops, Malcolm began his tuneless whistle – the sign he was at odds with himself.

The day we visited the Rhine Falls was a particularly long one, and followed a beer fest during which poor Chester was struck on the head by a porcelain stein with bas reliefs of pigs and grapes. Malcolm stood at the front of the bus with his microphone, telling us about the significant events of the Second World War which had occured in the vicinity, but almost all of the tour lolled in their seats – Chester with a little blood showing through his medical turban. I could see that Malcolm was mortified by the indifference to his commentary, and in-between battle sites his amplified whistle whined down the aisle, a sort of falsetto counterpoint to the rumblings of plumbing and snoring from the Wisconsin Foursome and others. Biological imperatives are stronger than manners, or the desire for educational instruction; Pierre continued to drive through the pleasant countryside we had all paid to see; Malcolm continued to provide his

When Gravity Snaps

commentary; the majority of the passengers slept with eyes closed and mouths open; Irene Hamble sidled towards the onboard lavatory.

The British conquered the world because they realized the benefit of a substantial breakfast. On three successive mornings in our Madrid hotel I ate only a small sugar bun. Nothing else was on offer. On that third morning we began the long trip to Lourdes, and I sat beside Glenda Waley who was barely fifty and recently widowed: her architect husband fell down the cellar steps in a client's partly finished Bristol home, striking the chassis of a 1927 Buick waiting there to be restored. Central Spain is very dry, with a lot of red earth, and for long distances nothing seemed to grow except olive trees. I didn't enjoy the views much, but the lack of eggs and toast may have been part of the reason. Glenda needed to tell me personal things about her dead husband – he had a benign enlargement of the prostate, she said, but was convinced he was dying, and he used to imitate his father in his sleep, talking dogmatically of Harold Wilson and the decline of English cricket. I felt sorry for Glenda, but even more so for her husband – he was dead, unable to keep up pretences any more, and his wife told strangers intimate things about his body and his inability to get free of his father.

'He'd hate it here,' said Glenda, as we drummed through the red heartland. 'He'd hate being pressed together on a tour bus like a school picnic. I couldn't consider coming until he'd passed on. He loved to be alone in a very large room, and said there was research about crowding rats together. That was one of his problems as an architect; he kept suggesting rooms larger than his clients could afford.' Glenda Waley was a serene, well groomed woman who got on well with us all, except Trevor. She always had an apple, or orange, for morning tea, and peeled it adroitly with a special tool, skin looping unbroken into her lap. I was only one of many who watched surreptitiously in car parks and scenic stops all over Europe for the tragedy of a discontinuity, but it never came. Glenda had some fine rings from the architectural earnings of her dead husband; my wife particularly admired a large sapphire in a raised setting surrounded by diamonds.

As we neared Bilbao the country was greener and more

productive. Malcolm told us of the ethnic and linguistic uniqueness of the Basques who lived in the area, and widow Waley laid a hand of glittering gems on my knee to reinforce the candidness with which she betrayed her husband's privacy. 'Glenn had an abhorrence of body hair,' she said. 'On himself, on anyone, but especially women. He wouldn't let me shave because of stubble and insisted on both of us using a clinically prescribed depilatory cream at least once a week. Esau is what he called hairy people. He was once physically ill after sitting beside a Hungarian professor of architectural history who had a full-face black beard that ran into his nostrils and ears.' Malcolm's voice, carrying a carefully balanced explanation of local terrorism, was a background to our conversation.

'Maybe his father was a hairy man,' I ventured. There is something of the amateur psychologist in us all. 'An Esau perhaps.'

'Not at all,' said Glenda Waley, 'but he used to beat Glenn with a dog collar which hung behind the scullery door.'

Whenever I read about the Basques now, they are in my mind's eye extremely hirsute people, flinging bombs and deeply hating their fathers. 'But I've been talking just about myself,' said Glenda. 'Very rude of me; you must tell me what you and your wife thought of the hotel in Madrid.'

On the island of Capri, Irene Hamble and the Dutch girl went missing. No one was sure if they had remained in Anacapri or taken the chair lift to the very top of the island as Malcolm suggested. How wonderful the chair lift was – quiet and private, flitting close over the garden terraces, rough grasses and small trees. At that height there was a cool breeze such as I hadn't felt for weeks, and in a vineyard which passed beneath I saw quite distinctly the dismembered pieces of several pink dolls lying among the green rows. Some juvenile Latin fury had been assuaged, I imagined, as had, with greater bloodshed, that of emperors so many years ago.

Malcolm asked us all to be on the lookout for Irene Hamble and the skinny girl, but I put them out of my mind and went to Axel Munthe's magnificent villa of San Michele at the foot of Mount Barbarossa. Irene Hamble was a born survivor with a

When Gravity Snaps

formidable nature apparent to any nationality; the Dutch girl would come to no harm with her, apart from obligatory sexual blandishments from local men because she was blonde.

I had read Munthe's great book as a student, and found it stirring and exotic. The content of his writing had long since leached from my mind, but I felt an odd frisson from the emotional associations of the villa. All sorts of antiquities were incorporated in the construction in eccentric ways, and I was lucky to come across Chester resting on the cool marble floor of a room which looked on to the shaded garden. Chester of course knew all the history of Capri, and most of that concerning the writer. He told me about Munthe being physician to the Swedish royal family, financing sanctuaries for migrating birds, living in Keats' house in Rome, visiting mad Guy de Maupassant, and having his sight restored by surgery after going blind. Such people seem to live heroic lives, while the rest of us have superannuation and ingrown toenails as topics of conversation.

While waiting for the Gambaegges at the top of the funicular, our party was rejoined by Irene Hamble and the Dutch girl, who claimed that Trevor had relayed garbled times concerning the day's activities. Only their tempers had suffered by their misadventure, but old Chester was inadvertently crushed by the Wisconsin Foursome while boarding the return ferry to Sorrento. He wasn't at dinner in the hotel that night, and my wife thought I should check up on him. I found him resting on his bed in shirt and sagging underpants, so his trousers wouldn't crease, in just the way I remember my father had done in his old age. Chester's legs were thin and white, and the knees were bulbous and wrinkled. His large nose seemed roughly modelled in clay and his mouth sagged open. The very appearance that age gives us is a form of indignity, but Chester's mind had suffered no atrophy and retained reach and power.

We had just opened a Chianti when Gillian Heading came to see how he was. I opened the door to her, and gave Chester enough time to pull a sheet across his lower half. 'No, no,' he said, 'I'm fine. It was just some bruising from the gangway, and after such a long, hot and wonderful day I thought I'd rest a little.'

'Those people are like elephants,' Gillian said.

Owen Marshall

'I'm sure Delmar and Blanche would have noticed me if they hadn't been talking.'

'Absolutely like elephants,' said Gillian. She was disappointed she'd chosen to go to the Blue Grotto rather than San Michele, and the more Chester told her of Axel Munthe the more certain was her conviction of loss. I could see that Chester was a little embarrassed at repeating the store of information he'd already shared with me earlier in the day, and though I would willingly have listened all over again, I made an excuse and went down to the bar. Trevor and Nick Guillermo had a table by the door, and Trevor began telling us about the maid on his floor who had an excellent arse and tits, and who was coming to his room after her shift.

The street between the hotel and the sea fell away steeply, and although I couldn't see Capri, above the blue neons of a pizza café was the dark, shifting shadow of the sea. Chester was perhaps telling Gillian of Axel Munthe's visit to Guy de Maupassant in the asylum at Passy. Maupassant was planting pebbles in the flower garden and told the creator of San Michele that the stones would grow into a host of little Maupassants when it rained. How Gillian would enjoy the story. While she talked with Chester, his legs palely naked beneath the sheet of modesty, she could forget she was redundant in the world of television.

There is a gold-roofed room in Innsbruck from which medieval ladies used to look down on the uncouth market throng in the town centre below, and not far from that is a small, secluded courtyard at the back of the old clock-tower, which has Hapsburg crests on its faces. I sat alone in the courtyard for more than an hour, and then a young gardener in a blue shirt came to weed the tiny plot around the fountain in the courtyard's centre. He looked up and smiled a good deal, and I could see that rather than concentrating on his work, he was curious as to my nationality. After a few minutes he gave up the pretence of work and spoke to me in English. He was studying economics at the university in Innsbruck, he said, and had a cousin working on an outback station in Queensland, but before we had talked long the sky darkened suddenly and there was a violent thunderstorm. Thunder, lightning and squalls of hailstones played about the old clock-tower. The gardener began to shout, but what I took at first

143

When Gravity Snaps

for exhilaration was fear, and he dropped the hoe, held his arms aloft to ward off a strike, and ran from the courtyard. His shirt had turned a much deeper blue in the rain, and he jumped the biggest puddles as he ran in an exaggerated, comic way. I took shelter in the clock-tower entrance, surprised that a young guy studying such a pragmatic subject as economics was afraid of lightning.

On the island of Burano, in the Venice lagoon, is a leaning spire. Mrs Guillermo came inside the church and translated some of the inscriptions and plaques for my wife and me, and Gillian Heading and Naomi Browne. The figurines were crudely made, but had a sort of glaring confidence. When back in the sun, Mrs Guillermo steered me aside and asked if I would spend more time with Nick, because she feared he was being unduly influenced by Trevor. How could I tell her that at Nick's age, and Trevor's, a preoccupation with sexual satisfaction is both natural and incorrigible.

Burano is famous for lace, and the beauty of it incited a shopping spree. At the café where we settled for lunch, the purchases were compared and praised. The Wisconsin wives had the most, but Glenda Waley had some of the most attractive lace, and she draped it on her smooth, hairless legs and arms for display. The rings from her dead husband glittered on the delicate material, and I thought how thankful he would be that she hadn't brought the shame of Esau on them, though the crowded tables would have been less agreeable for him. Those of the tour who could speak Italian – Mrs Guillermo, the Gibraltar Gambaegges, Malcolm, Chester, and to a lesser extent Nick and Gillian, made harmless fun with the waiters at the expense of the rest of us, and we tried to laugh off our ignorance.

After Fettucini Piccanti, and other courses of which only the flavours remain, my wife and I went outside with Chester, and sat by the bobbing small boats moored close to the café. They were painted with the colours of a merry-go-round: bright green, red, yellow and blue. We hoped for a breeze, which Chester said sometimes came in the evenings. He had been to the island twice before, and my wife asked him what differences he noticed when returning to places as he often had over the years. 'I began to think that my fellow travellers were more oafish each time,' he said, 'but now I realize I'm the one changing: gripped with the intolerance of old age.'

Chester had the habit of stroking the healing stein wound on his head, and the grey bristles above his ear rustled as he did so. It was pleasant to sit with an espresso and Barbera wine outside the café on Burano, and watch the twilight settling in. The Wisconsin Foursome could be heard discussing plumbing, and Trevor seemed to have offended a local woman, but it was all at a comforting remove inside the café. 'We'll send cards to each other for the first Christmas or two,' said Chester, 'and then exist only as increasingly uncertain images in the tour albums.'

'You must come and visit us,' said my wife emphatically.

'I will, I will,' agreed Chester.

A week or so before, as we discussed euthanasia in the foyer of a diamond workshop in Amsterdam, Chester told me that although he hadn't got quite the role he preferred in life, he would act out the whole play. In youth we mount the Pegasus of our ambition, and awake in old age astride a Shetland pony with our feet resting on the ground.

Chester was right as always: the night brought a breeze which whispered through the coloured boats of Burano, perhaps exhalations from the Bridge of Sighs itself, and Mrs Gambaegge began singing in Italian in the café behind us. Her husband joined in, and their unaccustomed harmony excused all the times they had kept us waiting, and gave hope for their marriage. An elderly woman stopped to listen, hunched in her doorway like a ruffled thrush. Chester raised the empty wine bottle to a waiter as a signal for a full replacement, and made my wife laugh softly with a whispered opinion of Trevor. It was one of those rare, serene and self-sufficient moments in our passage to the grave when there seemed a complete integration of spirit and external things. So let it be.

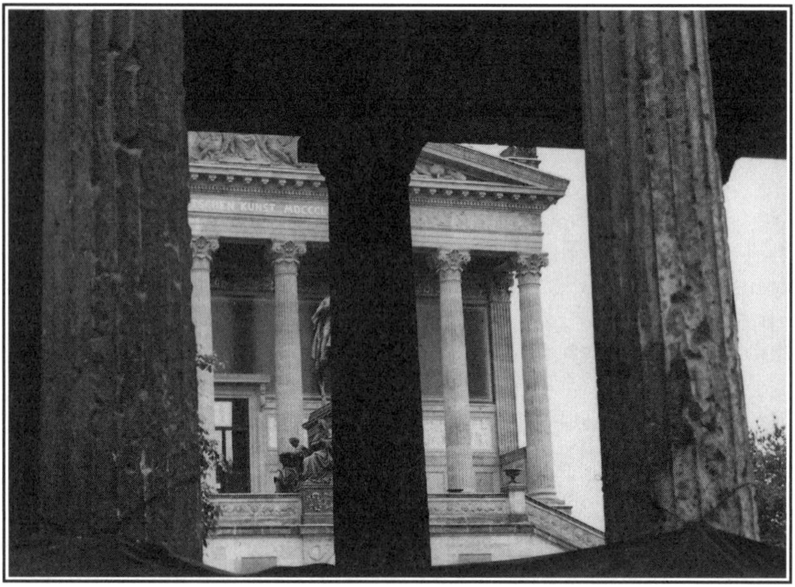
KUNST

Laura (Riding) Jackson
Other Creatures
Besides Ourselves . . .

This untitled, undated piece was probably intended by Laura (Riding) Jackson for inclusion in one of her yet-to-be-published books. Most likely it was composed in the late 1970s or early 1980s. It appears here by permission of the Laura (Riding) Jackson Board of Literary Management, and with the additional permission of the owners of the typescript and the manuscript: respectively, the Division of Rare and Manuscript Collections, Cornell University Library, and the Berg Collection of English and American Literature, the New York Public Library, Astor, Lenox, and Tilden Foundations.

Other creatures besides ourselves form unions of life-activity, adhere to patterns of behavior and performance that assure – have been found to assure for long – their survival as the kind of creatures they are. We human beings have formed our unions of living together with one another not as patterns centered to a commonly felt will to survive, but as patterns centered to a commonly felt will to know ourselves as what we are in the containing whole in which we are. It is our peculiar will, not just to live, perpetuate ourselves as the kind of beings we are, but to live according to the felt will of the containing whole. This will is felt as an indivisible definition of the right, comprehending which we cannot stray from the reality of the all-embracing place or the reality of ourselves in it: we live forever in its forever. This right is the first believed-in of the human mind.

In all early unions of living together of human beings, an image of the right, elevated to commanding truth-height, presided as an immortalizing law of human existence. It is our special nature to

Other Creatures Besides Ourselves ...

want to know and understand aright, do right, say rightly, to compose our minds to treating the choices that distinguish themselves for our making as falling under one principle of judgement; to view all that we experience from our minds, bring it into a single view, not to rest at apprehending it in separate experiences of sight or other modes of sensation, or in the mingled modes of sensation called 'impressions', or in eccentric ('subjective') private-mindedness.

We are so made as to be able to think ourselves into the actual realness of our nature as beings having mind of an all-containing being-presence, *its* nature that of a mind it has of itself as all of one realness, indivisibly. And in the continual change after change through which human life has travelled, in its times and places, as a mind-instructed way of being – from crude (and cruel!) conceptions of a master-totality, all-ruling rightness, binding fast act to act, idea to idea, belief to belief, to later and later refinements of mind-vigilance loosening the strings of thought-obedience – there has prevailed an unchanging constant of adherence to a *prior* consciousness of the centeredness of human life to a living whole, a being-entirety – what has been designated, in philosophical laboratory language, 'reality'. I mean: *the reality* – the real all-happening we know in knowing ourselves really to be.

There has prevailed an overhanging consciousness of the reality *until* this time of ours. In all the changes in how human beings have lived under the tutorship of their minds, not until *this* time have their minds closed out the primordial human apprehension – the mind's first acquaintance with itself as mind in its first acquaintance with the knowable as an indivisible all-to-know.

How does the adventuring of now in more and more kinds of knowledge, thinking in terms of experience of more and more kinds of 'reality', make up for the unitary reality that has come to be excluded from intellectual legitimacy – from the status of truth – as mere ritual of arguable hypothesis or mere substance of belief (ignorance mixed with knowledge, knowledge with ignorance, in proportions satisfying the mind for the time being)? Not only does the abundance of new knowledge not make up for the at last discarded uncomfortable treasure of early intuitions of an all-to-know, prolonged in their hoarded scantiness until we decided to free our minds from the errors of history by separating ourselves from ourselves: this new human-mindedness converts the human being into a something else where there is nothing else to be but an animal being with the brain of a human being, the mind as the seat of human identity nullified as such, absorbed into the animal brain as an enlargement of it with intricately self-duplicating processes of memory of *human* behavior.

The casting, now, of human beings of themselves in the rôle of beings of human identity, in individual consciousness and on the social ground of intellectual activity, is becoming, with rapid envelopment of all the distinctively human concerns, a computerized brain record, a memory-model. The energies of conscious being that *are* mind, that directly link the being possessed of them with the totality of being in its indivisible realness, its self-insistence as the Right, the truth of truths, have been, are being, sucked back into the site of materially organic human existence – the brain area – at a rate of dissipation of them that seems to be coming closer and closer to the irreversible. The names of the ageless forms of our manifestation of our humanity have not changed, but the forms are diluted with uncertainty as to what inheres of particular meaning in being alive *humanly*. Our manifestation of our humanity has become formless. Only the names of the historic human practices remain; the confounding of practice with practice transmutes the quality 'human' into a quantity – and new names are added to the old, and the make-up of human life and knowledge ceases to be an unvarying matter of substance, is a continually revised question of vocabulary. All is kept in a play of redefinition. There is religion, philosophy, science, history, literature, poetry, art. But there is no longer a continuity of faith in there being an all-over right reason for the existence of human beings – a fated human concern with the right – holding these practices to an unchanging objective of honor-paying, in their varying manner as forms of human truth-recognition, to an unchanging meaning, original and ultimate, of universal existence.

The dawning of the twentieth century as a new millennial day of the human mind brought human life into the light of a new order of intelligence of existence, which had been building itself

Other Creatures Besides Ourselves . . .

up in the precursory shades of what has come to be called 'modern time' – in the sophistications of Renaissance and post-Renaissance humanistic personalism. I have come to regard this new order of intelligence as a power assumed by the human mind to treat itself as an object of suspicion to itself. The twentieth-century version of the human mind disavows its character as a given condition of elementarily general knowledge. It teaches itself that it knows nothing – that it must begin to know all over again. It dispossesses itself of the primordial order of intelligence, which begins with the sense of totality, revising the natural movement of human understanding as from general to particularized consciousness: the sense of totality, which is the mind's spiritual *vade mecum*, is overwhelmed in processes of expansion of particular knowledge, augmentation of particularities of experience within the compass of delimited fields of knowledge. A sense of triviality becomes the *vade mecum* of the mind. The mind is no longer, for the twentieth-century human being, the reality of *human* identity, evidence of its spiritual practicality; it is an implement of heightened physical self-awareness, consciousness of human identity as a curiosity in a universe full of curiosities.

Why, why, have human beings translated human identity into an animal-exceeding animal extraordinariness? Was it because the constant of consciousness of a principle of rightness embracing the whole actuality of varied being in one all-simplifying truth became an embarrassment to human minds grown too busy with mounting enlargements of knowledge-detail and multiplication of experience-detail for reflecting on a single certainty, holding everything together? Did the minds, succeeding in knowing more and more, probing into more and more quarters of special knowledge, come to view the reason of minds, their inspiring cause, as a distraction from their developed special purposes? Have the minds moved out of the natural universe into a universe composed of their voluminous knowledge-exploits – into a maturity that is a stranger to its youth, and to itself?

The universe of twentieth-century human consciousness is the world of beings living outside themselves. The minds that have created it, from animal vanity in their humanness, have lost their grandeur as human minds. Human minds, by their nativity, are partakers of the genius of the universe – its inner reality to itself, its mind-containment of itself within its great trying-out of the limits of the illimitable: they are the express consequence of its care against the dissolution of excess, the effective limits of its being the all of being. But twentieth-century human beings fell into self-excess – they have ceased to know themselves as the mind-creatures of the universe. They know a universe that is a widening spread of many knowledges – and the more knowledges, the more parted is one knowledge from another: in these pluralities their very powers of knowledge are dispersed. They piece together a totality they inhabit only as a convention of common human consciousness; it is little more than a common state of mind of total uncertainty. They inhabit only their own minds, the mind of each a private universe, and each special knowledge is a truth resortable to against the insufficiency as truth of another special knowledge, or all the others together. And the private personal universes collide with one another in a meeting of minds that is but an exercise in rough comparison at the distance of common language made the secret tool of each mind's private universe of understanding.

How, then, have they, you, we, succeeded in getting along – in keeping themselves all, yourselves all, *us*, what is called 'going'? By pretending that nothing has changed, that we still regard ourselves as existing under the universal dispensation by which there were, are, human beings, witnesses of the whole there is to know, though preferring not to press the point. You have, the contemporary we have, divested us all, as we are datedly human, of our born character of witnesses of the whole there is to know, by grace of mind fulfilling its peace with itself in sense of the Right implicit in its all-apparent self-faithful entireness. Your minds argue this and that to be the Right without having any reverence for the idea of a Right. You desecrate the explicit nature of us, and the implicit nature of the whole course of being. You treat the given totality as if it were your real world only in a vaguely concrete allusiveness. It has become an abstraction; science-fiction dehumanizes rather than humanizes the abstraction. You treat the human past as a stock-in-trade for

Other Creatures Besides Ourselves . . .

present-day intellectual commerce, in the manner of experts in all things human, while reducing the human future to a negotiable extension of the past. You have brought your minds to standstill in the human function of honoring the indivisible spirit of universal being, knowable to human beings from its unreserved presence in themselves, the sense of the whole their enjoyable good, their followable Right, their speakable truth.

Poet Laura Riding (1901-1991) worked first in her native USA, where she was associated with the Fugitives, then in Europe, with some collaboration with Robert Graves among others. She renounced poetry in about 1941, having come to judge it an artificial substitute for natural truth-speaking. There followed two decades devoted to the study of language with her husband Schuyler Jackson, issuing in the crowning three decades of renewedly prolific writing and publishing activity, most notably The Telling *(1972). A number of her books are available from Carcanet (Manchester) and Persea Books (New York); several of her earlier works have recently been republished, and two unpublished books are due to appear in 2003.* The Laura (Riding) Jackson Reader *and the authorised biography by Elizabeth Friedmann should be available in 2004.*

Douglas Cowie
My Smokestack

Tin smokestack me – I – see out window from my room. Smokestack. No smoke. Nobody home. Where they go now? Tree or sea and wind and my smokestack. Man come soon and say, Hello today you are how? How are? And I get food then also. In dark, at night, I put face to window and squint hard and see tin smokestack. Never smoke. Morning man come, say, Good morning today! And me, I clap and say, Today! Smokestack! Sometime he say, Out of pajamas, you, put on clothes and coat and hat, and then he and me, we go sea with others. I like my pajamas. It's warm. And sand. I don't swim. I try from sea to look my smokestack and it not there. But I at home in my room, in pajamas, then I see and it's OK, then, OK. I sleep. And morning it there once more, again, but no smoke, and it's OK. One time lady come, say, Hello, boy mine! Are you OK, hello? I know, I say her back, I know, looking at smokestack. Like you new pajamas I bring? Ask she, but I don't know, so I look my smokestack, out window. Like it, smokestack. Then also man come, again, and ask me how today. I shrug. Sometime he put to shoulder his hand and say, Try, and I don't know what and I say, Smokestack, look, point. Smokestack never on, though. Never no any smoke in it, from it, the smokestack from my window. Once a bird, though, on it, and then man come in, he say, What how today, hello? And I turn, point out window, say, Bird, smokestack, on it today, but he say, What? And I try again, Bird on it, out the window, my smokestack, pointing, but when he look, he say, No, not there, so I point, look, but yes, it away, the bird out my smokestack window I see then there today, no then, that day, on the, on my

My Smokestack

smokestack, of course. And then that day, another one, he and she and another and one more, when I'm in pajamas and looking my smokestack, no bird, they come, say, Hello, today! Surprise for you, for me, they tell me, today, that day, and, New Room! they say, and I say, Smokestack, too, but they say nothing but, New Room! Nicer! And I look, going, with them, him, her and two, out window, to see, because New Room, I thought, I think, then I thought, think now, then, won't have it, it will not, the new room will not have the same smokestack, or any. Smokestack. It does not have one. I looked, and I live there, with a window, but nothing. Not a smokestack. Not my smokestack. Not any. Window has nothing, and now when he comes I say nothing, having no smokestack, or nothing to say.

But back I go, want to, to go, I want back to my smokestack to go, on other side. Draw time, Art call it they, Art let's make, they say what. But it draw, only. Paper, and wax colors and we draw, all, me, he and he and he and others. Many, all. We draw. And they, man and others, come, say, Good draw! Nice, how! But it always same draw, I draw. Now, especially. Draw smokestack. And hang they best ones on walls in big room. Picture there of smokestack. My smokestack draw. Today, or before, or later, remember can't I, new draw, add bird, and me, smokestack on top. On top of the, on top of my smokestack. Man come, say, Hey! That there, what, on smokestack top? Bird, say I, bird and also other, me, there, smokestack on top. See from there, say. But he wrinkle eyes, say, How, what, on top? Sense make it? So I shrug and draw new, again, smokestack, on top, crown, me, king, but don't show it man, I don't, no, not to him. Pocket, keep, to later look and see.

Night, before, no, later, same, maybe, or other, don't know, I take from pocket, in room, one without it, without the, the room without my smokestack I am in, from pocket take the picture, the one, me, with smokestack and crown. King. Look, in dark, at it. Have to put nose close, to see, although eyes, not nose, what does it, the looking. Smile, then, I at the picture, in the dark, but hear steps, it time when man come, say, Ready, lights for bed off, hello? So quickly I into pillowcase put and he come and not see it, when.

Douglas Cowie

Next day, or later, but earlier, no, later, probably, it that time, man come, say, Sea today, hello, ready, get! And I shrug. Pajamas wear to the sea, always, I, but today, no, not, because no pocket. I pocket need for picture, and also other.

So, to sea. Close, but always long drive they make us. Down to one side, then back way we came, but different road. Why, to confuse I don't know maybe. When I stand ready in big room, not pajamas with, man come, say, Good, pajamas no! Learn something we, yes, hello! And smile, he, so me, too, smile also. When turn he, to others talk, on other side, pat I pocket, mine, with picture, and other.

I tell: in pocket, picture, yes, I said, but also other. Other: wax color I steal, and back of picture white, with nothing.

We into car, no, truck, no, bus, they, the man and his others, they say bus always. Small bus, but enough big for me. I first go in, to back, in corner by window. I need window. I need back, me, for not to see, for they, the man, and his others, to not see. I watch. Others, like me, they come into bus and sit other places. Not by mine, by me, where I sit. Others sit never by mine, when I there I sit, but OK, that's, me, with especially today. I plan.

And bus goes, and I watch. Front, where sit man and his others, not looking back, me, where sit. So wax color out, red, OK. I make X middle. And then line, while drive bus, and when it turn, the bus, when the bus turn, I also, with red, on paper, back of picture, where was white, when then the bus turns, so do I, but on the paper, with the red, with the red wax color. Careful I make it, so right, yes, but also, not to see, for the others. So they see other things, but not me, what I do. And bus turn, so me, I turn again, on the paper, with the red. And also I watch, after, when another road, so I can also make a line there, after the bus turn, another line, to count, so I know. And each time, another line, and the turn, also the line, all the way to the sea, and there, another X, and to make different, on first X I make, fast, a, the, I make fast my smokestack there, on the X, so different, to remember, not to know, but to remember, because already of course I know, so they're different, the two X, and an arrow to the top also I draw, from the sea away. Then quickly into pocket, both, paper, picture side and now new other, but wax color I put also, to get rid of.

My Smokestack

And sea I stand, usual, always stand, not swim, but man let me, OK, so nobody watch, or notice, I stand, not wet in sea, the picture, and also its new other side, but OK, because never, so nobody tell, and I, me, safe, looking, like always, at, no, for, because not see, the, my smokestack. But also think, remember bus turns, and red turns, and also X and other X. Remember, and think, so wait, and also look for my smokestack.

And back we go, and I pat my pocket, with picture and other, and then I smile and sit inside bus, to look once more the window out, to remember, again, but new, to remember also not just the red lines I draw but also how it see with buildings and other, because it not only a red line, or road. At night, then, or, no, later, at night, but the same, I check red lines on other side my picture and remember how each looks to see at, so when later.

Morning next no sea, but I pat my pocket three times that day. Sea must be patient because only sometimes there he, man and his others, take me, and others, he and he and he and others, not no every time, every day, so patient, until next time. Next time though, when, not sure, but later, anyway, than next day or next, later sometime, I think, but not earlier, yes, no, not earlier, later, this next time, though, no good, because no chance. On way to sea I look on other side to make sure I wrote is right way, or way isn't different this time. It all look same, though, good, I smile, and pocket, into it I put back the picture with its other side, and I pat it, and smile again, once more. At sea, then, that time, I stand and watch, and look, like always. He and he and he and others, and the man and his others, all in sea, I hear, behind me, splash and yell and laugh, they all are there in the sea, except for the one him, the one he, who they keep tie to bar, to not run away, into sea, because not swim, can't, he, that one, tied up. Then I think, for next time, because now too late, this time, but later, I earlier try, think, next time I know that earlier I can what do, if I remember, must I remember. To not forget, I look around and nobody not watching me, so I take wax color, careful from pocket and also picture, with its other side, and then I look again, but nobody seeing, so I careful write word down, I write down, careful, Remember. Then I remember, the next time, later, to be earlier to look, and act. Quickly back into pocket then everything, or both, wax color, and picture with its other side, I put it all, both back inside the pocket, my pocket, and pat it, and smile. Ready, then, for next time, when later it comes. I'll be earlier, and because I will remember, having written down, Remember. Remember.

Much much later, then, finally, come the day. Much later because so much water, so much rain, all every day, and no sea. So some day they say, tomorrow sea, but tomorrow, the next day, they say, No, can't, because rain, it, no we can't go to sea, and I pat my pocket, sad, but wait, and remember, to not forget, that I wrote down that word. Remember. But, already I said, that day come, then, finally, and sun, and he, the man, with others, smile in morning, say, Today, hello! Sea we can, all the way, because not rain, and sun, so today, we can! And I pat my pocket and smile, ready.

And we go, in bus, I sit in back alone, and watch, just road, and next to it, to the roads, buildings, my red lines I can see without looking at where I drew them on other side of my picture, and I smile, to sea, on the way, watching, knowing. And everything is right, in my thought, and what I see, it all the same, and I don't even need the word I wrote down, the one, because I already think, I already remember, having written it down.

At sea all out they go, the others, and the man and his, and me at last, and I stand where always, and pat my pocket, and watch as they, the man and others, put rope to bar for him, the one, who doesn't swim, and then I watch them to the sea, and then I turn. I hear them, the splash, the laugh, and then I know I'm ready so I look and yes I'm ready, because they, splash and swim in sea, but not look. Not at me.

I go to he, to him, the one who doesn't swim, and look the rope at his arm and to the bar. He smile and laugh, say, Me! Yes! I go! And I put finger to lips, Shhh. He smile and nod, and I untie. When rope not attached at bar, he run towards sea, and I only watch fast, once, quickly, before run in right direction, while pulling picture, with other red lines on its side, out of my pocket, and down the road, where I stop to run, but keep going, walk, look not strange. I check map, and look road, and its buildings, and smile, because it all look right. I hear, behind, voices, I hear

My Smokestack

man, say, William! But William not me, William him who tied up, so I know, OK, time, it will not be until later, so I walk, but maybe faster, and I check red lines I that time made, although no, I remember, so don't need.

Nobody in street to see or ask, so I feel OK, and follow careful the way back. Not far, because I notice, earlier when we came, I saw that other streets can be used, not the way the bus goes, long, but a short way, back to where I can be, where I have a room, and where the old room, with the, with my smokestack, the old room with my smokestack out window is. And soon I get to there, to that place, and I then look at other side, not red lines, but other, first, where there I had once drew picture, in wax colors, of it, of the, of my smokestack and with me, with crown, me the King there on top. Careful I go around, in case somebody see and then all no good, close to the wall I go around, to where I think it is, the, my smokestack.

And I get there. I see above where my window used to be, where it still, now, there it is, but not mine, no, because they put me in other place, without a, without the smoke, without my smokestack. And there it is. My smokestack. I look again my drawing and now I go to it, to my smokestack. The picture back into my pocket, to be safe, I put it there. I put one hand on my smokestack, first time, and smile. Then other. I squeeze it, my smokestack, so not to let go, or to fall. Then lift. Hard, to lift, but I put foot and then other foot on bottom of my smokestack, and then a little easier, and soon halfway to top, one hand, then other hand, then two feet, at same time, up, up, up, careful and smiling, and also sweat, but up, and then, at top, I can see, I hold arms around my smokestack, and legs too, and I can see, look over at the sea. Just almost, from up there, because my head above my smokestack, and from the sea I couldn't see it, my smokestack, but from my smokestack I can see the sea. People there, the others, he and the other hes, and also the man and his others, and I see them make circles on sand, and I hear, quiet, voices, above wind and water. They look, I know, for me. I know. I wave, arm high, but of course, they look on sand, and not for me at my smokestack. When I had crown, then could I be my picture, the one I made, before the red lines that brought me here. I reach careful to pocket and take it, unfold with mouth and hand to look again. And smile. I am my picture. On other side I wrote Remember, and on this side I have picture of me, and my smokestack. And now I have me and my smokestack together, not just picture. I sit, holding, legs around my smokestack, and wave picture to sea, and nobody look, though.

How long, I don't know, I there, and then they come back, the others, all of them, without me, to find me, maybe, if they look, but maybe I'm lost, is what they think. I am not lost. I am here, on top of my smokestack, if they want to see. I hear my name calling out, though, when I see bus come, it goes shorter, I notice, as I watch, not the way of usual, but faster, straight from sea to here, where I am sitting on top of my smokestack. They all out then, and man and his others run around and the others, like me, them, they follow behind, yelling also, like the man and his others, who are all yelling. They come to my smokestack, to my smokestack, where I sit, and they all yell, and wave, from up down, like they say, Come down, here, and they say my name out, but I wave back and show my picture, here, my King picture, me here on top of my smokestack just like the King, me, the King on top of my smokestack, but then the man, he start to try to climb my smokestack but no, I won't, not on my smokestack, he can't climb because it is not his it is my smokestack, and I won't let him climb my smokestack and I spit, down there, but miss, it goes by side, but he see and look up, scowl and shout angry something, but still climb, so I spit again, and hit, in his face as he looks, and then he say, OK, hello that the end, mister, but I don't know, so I shout, Smokestack, my smokestack, and spit again and then he's getting closer, so I wave my picture again, and spit again, and then I think, if not my smokestack only, not his either, my smokestack I don't want him on my smokestack, so I spit, wave, look, all them there, down, yell and jump and he comes closer and out to the sea I look once more, spit, look, wave, and then I jump, and as I jump from my smokestack I see the sea one last, and I see my picture, the one, and the red lines, too, from my hand and up, I see me, the King, on top of my smokestack, my smokestack, no more.

What do I want to accomplish as *The Georgia Review* editor?

The answer to that is clear: I want to edit this magazine in such a way that excellent writing will come into being that would not have existed had I and the staff not done this work. This is the best thing a journal can do—be a catalyst that enables or provokes writers to write beyond themselves.

— T.R. Hummer

Each issue of *The Georgia Review* features some 200 pages of fine writing, as well as a visual art portfolio—usually in full color. Writers range from Nobel laureates and Pulitzer Prize winners to the most deserving newer voices. Here you will regularly find distinctive writing that invites and sustains repeated readings. Available in fine bookstores for $9 per copy or by subscription in the U. S. for $24/year (four issues). Subscriptions in all other countries are $30/year.

The Georgia Review

The University of Georgia, Athens, GA 30602-9009
(706) 542-3481 • garev@uga.edu
Please visit our web site at www.uga.edu/garev.

Biographical Notes

Ammiel Alcalay is a poet, translator, critic and scholar. His latest work, *from the warring factions* (Beyond Baroque, 2002), is a book length poem dedicated to the Bosnian town of Srebrenica. His translations include *Sarajevo Blues* by Bosnian poet Semezdin Mehmedinović (City Lights, 1998), and *Keys to the Garden: New Israeli Writing* (City Lights, 1996).

Joshua Beckman's collections of poetry include *Something I Expected to Be Different* (Verse Press, 2001) and *Things Are Happening* (1998), which was selected by Gerald Stern to receive the first American Poetry Review/Honickman First Book Award. He has had work published in *Harper's*, *Grand Street*, and *Massachusetts Review*. He now lives in New York City.

Thomas Brussig was born in Berlin in 1965, grew up in the Eastern section of the city and after graduating from school worked as, among other things, a furniture mover and a museum and hotel porter. He studied sociology and drama and in 1991 published his debut novel under a pseudonym. In 1995 his novel *Helden Wie Wir* (*Heroes Like Us*), which has been translated into numerous languages and adapted as a play, was published. In 1999 he received, along with Leander Haussmann, the '*Drehbuchpreis der Bundesregierung*' (German Government Screenplay Prize). Thomas Brussig lives in Berlin. 'The Condemned' is the second chapter of his novel, *Am kürzeren Ende der Sonnenallee* (*On the Short End of Sunnyside Lane*).

Douglas Cowie was born in Elmhurst, Illinois. His stories have appeared in *Magpie*, *White Noise* and the *New Delta Review*. He currently divides his time between Norwich and Berlin.

Biographical Notes

Aleš Debeljak, poet and essayist, is a director of the Center for Cultural and Religious Studies at the University of Ljubljana, Slovenia. He has won several awards, including the Slovenian National Book Award, the Miriam Lindberg Israel Poetry for Peace Prize (Tel Aviv) and Chiqu Poetry Prize (Tokyo). His recent publications in English include *Reluctant Modernity*, *Twilight of the Idols: Recollections of a Lost Yugoslavia* and three books of poems: *Anxious Moments*, *The City and the Child* and *Dictionary of Silence*. He is the general editor of the book series *Terra Incognita: Writings from Central Europe*, published by White Pine Press, Buffalo, New York.

Ben Faccini was born in England and brought up in France and Italy. He worked for many years at the United Nations in Paris. He now lives in London. In 2002, he published his first novel, *The Water-Breather*.

Anne Green is a Senior Lecturer in German at Carnegie Mellon University, interested in materials development and curriculum enhancement, particularly through use of the Web and of German children's and youth literature. Anne met Thomas Brussig in 1997 and organized several reading tours for him in the USA. This is her first translation of a novel.

Aleksandar Hemon was born in Sarajevo, Bosnia-Herzegovina, where he lived until he ended up in Chicago in 1992. He has been writing short stories in English since 1995. His stories have appeared in *TriQuarterly*, *Ploughshares*, *The New Yorker*, *The Baffler*, *Granta*, *Esquire*, *The Paris Review* and in the *Best American Short Stories* 1999 and 2000. He is the author of *The Question of Bruno* (2000) and *Nowhere Man* (2002) both by Picador. He lives in Chicago.

Ana Jelnikar teaches English and translates extensively both into Slovenian and English. Many of her translations of Slovenian poets have been published in foreign literary magazines, especially in America (*Verse*, *Southern Humanities Review*, *Third Coast*, and *The American Poetry Review*). She is also the translator of the first Slovenian edition of C.G. Jung's *Man and His Symbols*. She lives in Ljubljana, Slovenia.

Owen Marshall is a New Zealander. He has published and edited eighteen books. Owen received the ONZM for services to literature in the Queen's New Year's Honours, 2000, and in the same year his novel, *Harlequin Rex*, won the Deutz Medal for fiction at the Montana New Zealand Book Awards. In 2002

Biographical Notes

the University of Canterbury awarded him the honorary degree of Doctor of Letters. A collection of stories, *When Gravity Snaps*, is his latest publication.

Colum McCann is the author of two short story collections and three novels, most recently *Dancer*. In 2002 he won the inaugural Princess Grace Memorial Award for Fiction. His work has been published in fifteen languages. He currently lives in New York.

Semezdin Mehmedinović, born in Bosnia in 1960, is the author of four books, including *Sarajevo Blues* (City Lights, 1998). In 1993 he was co-writer and co-director, together with Benjamin Filipović, of *Mazaldo*, one of the first Bosnian films shot during the war. The film was presented at the Berlin Film Festival in 1994, and won the first prize at the Mediterranean Festival in Rome the following year. He, his wife and their son left Bosnia and came to the US as political refugees in 1996. He remained a citizen of Sarajevo throughout the Serbian nationalists' siege and was active in the city's resistance movement. He is a translator for the 'Voice of America'.

Christopher Merrill is a poet, translator, editor and essayist. *Watch Fire* received the Peter I. B. Lavan Younger Poets Award from the Academy of American Poets. He has translated Aleš Debeljak's *Anxious Moments* and *The City and the Child*; and his books of non-fiction include *Only the Nails Remain: Scenes from the Balkan Wars*. His work has been translated into twelve languages. He directs the International Writing Program at The University of Iowa.

Claire Messud is the author of *When the World was Steady*, a finalist for the PEN/Faulkner Award, and *The Last Life*. Her latest book is *The Hunters*.

Jens Mühling was born in Siegen, Germany, in 1976. He studied Comparative Literature in Berlin and Norwich, and has worked as a journalist in Germany, England and Russia. Currently he lives in Berlin and works as a freelance journalist, his main field being the arts.

Stef Pixner published a volume of poetry, *Sawdust and White Spirit* (Virago). She is working on a collection of short stories and lives in London.

Peter Richards is a poet and translator, and a graduate of the Iowa Writers' Workshop.

Biographical Notes

Laura (Riding) Jackson Please see page 152 for details.

Michèle Roberts is half-English and half-French. She is the author of eleven novels, three collections of poetry, and two of short stories, most recently *Playing Sardines* (Virago, 2002). Her most recent novel is *The Mistressclass* (Little, Brown, 2003). Her novel *Daughters of the House* was shortlisted for the Booker Prize in 1992 and won the WH Smith Literary Award in 1993. She is Professor of Creative Writing at UEA.

Tomaž Šalamun writes in Slovenian, lives in Ljubljana, at the moment in Berlin, and occasionally teaches in the US. He's widely translated and anthologized. His last two books in English translation are *Feast* (Harcourt, 2000) and *A Ballad for Metka Krasovec* (Twisted Spoon Press, 2001). His *Selected Poems* edited by Charles Simic and introduced by Robert Hass were published in England by ARC Publishers as *Homage to Hat & Uncle Guido & Eliot* in 1997.

W.G. Sebald Please see page 25 for details.

Rachel Seiffert's first novel, *The Dark Room*, was shortlisted for the 2001 Booker Prize, and she has also received an *LA Times* Prize and an International PEN Award for her work. Rachel has recently been included in *Granta*'s Best of Young British Novelists 2003. *Dimitroff* will be published by William Heinemann in 2004 as part of a new collection of short stories.

George Szirtes was born in Budapest and came to England as a refugee. He was trained as an artist. He has written some dozen books of poetry, most recently *The Budapest File* (2000) and *An English Apocalypse* (2001) and has translated poetry, fiction and drama from the Hungarian. His work has won several awards, most recently a Leverhulme Fellowship and a Society of Authors Travelling Scholarship.

Jono Tosch is a photographer and writer. He lives and works in Bloomington, Indiana. He writes and publishes the comedy fanzine *Idiot Hero*.

Andrew Wachtel is Bertha and Max Dressler Professor in the Humanities and Chair of the Department of Slavic Languages and Literatures at Northwestern University. A prolific translator from Russian, Bulgarian, Croatian, Serbian and Slovenian, he published most recently, with Anastassis Vistonitis, *At the Crossroads: New Writing from South East Europe* (Athens, 2002).

Reactions

Volume 4
Edited by Esther Morgan

Reactions[4] is another round-up of the best new poets from around the UK and abroad. Reactions features the work of poets who are at a first collection stage or working towards it.

Buying is easy . . .

For ONLY £7.99 (inc. p&p) per issue you get Reactions delivered direct to your door. Send a cheque payable to the University of East Anglia, to the address below. **Reactions**[4] is available **October 2003** from all good bookshops priced £7.99 ISBN: 1-902913-18-3

REACTIONS • VOLUMES 1 & 2 • £6 EACH

REACTIONS 3 — £7.99

Pen & Inc Press
English & American Studies
University of East Anglia
Norwich, Norfolk, NR4 7TJ, UK
info@penandinc.co.uk
+44 (0)1603 592783

www.penandinc.co.uk

SUBMISSION GUIDELINES 2003/2004

Pen & Inc Press is based at the University of East Anglia. It publishes a literary review, **Pretext**, which includes poetry, fiction, non-fiction and criticism, and **Reactions**, a poetry anthology for poets at first collection stage.

PRETEXT SUBMISSION GUIDELINES

Pretext is published twice a year in May and November. Each issue of **Pretext** is guest edited by a writer of distinction, who is invited to solicit about half of his or her issue, with the other half coming from the Managing Editor, the **Pretext** editorial board and unsolicited manuscripts. **Pretext 8** (November 2003) will be guest edited by Helon Habila (*Waiting for an Angel*).

We publish short stories, poetry, essays and non-fiction, and we are looking for:

- Original short fiction (maximum length 6,000 words), poetry (a maximum of five poems), essays on writers or on writing (please submit ideas/synopses to the editors in the first instance), personal essays/memoirs.

- Please submit all work typed in a plain legible font and double-spaced with address printed on each page. Cover letter or a brief intro is fine.

- The payment is £50 for accepted publication in **Pretext**.

- Submissions should be made by post only. **Faxes and emails are not accepted.** Please don't send computer disks.

- Please let us know if your work is being published elsewhere during this time.

- We do not send out acknowledgement letters.

- Timing: we aim to respond in three months. However, due to the volume of work to be considered, we have regularly exceeded this time span so be prepared for a potentially long wait. We do respond to every manuscript eventually.

- Enclose a Stamped Addressed Envelope or an International Reply Coupon if you are outside the UK. Please indicate (and enclose sufficient postage) if you would like your work returned.

- Submissions for **Pretext** should be sent to: Katri Skala, Pretext, Pen & Inc Press, School of English and American Studies, University of East Anglia, Norwich, Norfolk, NR4 7TJ, UK.

DEADLINES FOR SUBMISSIONS TO *PRETEXT* ARE END OF JANUARY & END OF JULY

Reactions Submission Guidelines

Reactions is published annually in October. Submissions are invited from writers who have had a first collection or pamphlet published (but not a second) and from those who have not yet reached that stage. Basically, the focus is on new talent.

- Submissions must be your own original work. It can be on any subject, in any style and of any length.

- Maximum of five poems.

- Submissions should be written in English, but can be translations.

- Please submit all work typed in a plain legible font and with address printed on each page.

- Any submission must be accompanied by a covering letter that lists the titles of your poems, plus a short biography of no more than 70 words.

- The payment is £50 for accepted publication in **Reactions**.

- Your submission must not have been accepted for publication in any magazine (although poems due to appear in a first collection or anthology will be considered.)

- Please let us know if your work is being published elsewhere during this time.

- Submissions should be made by post only. **Faxes and emails are not accepted.** Please don't send computer disks.

- We do not send out acknowledgement letters.

- Timing: we aim to respond in three months. However, due to the volume of work to be considered, we have regularly exceeded this time span, so be prepared for a potentially long wait. We do respond to every manuscript eventually.

- Enclose a Stamped Addressed Envelope or an International Reply Coupon if you are outside the UK. Please indicate (and enclose sufficient postage) if you would like your work returned.

- Submissions for **Reactions** should be sent to: Esther Morgan, Pen & Inc Press, School of English and American Studies, University of East Anglia, Norwich, Norfolk, NR4 7TJ, UK.

Deadline for submissions to *Reactions* 5 is 31 March 2004

PUBLICATIONS

Pretext, Reactions, MA Creative Writing Anthology, Writers in Conversation

For details of all currently available titles from Pen & Inc Press, please contact us:

> Pen & Inc Press
> School of English & American Studies
> University of East Anglia
> Norwich, Norfolk, NR4 7TJ, UK
> info@penandinc.co.uk
> +44 (0)1603 592783

The Arvon Foundation

Committed to encouraging creative writing and supporting creative writers.

Arvon Courses offer a dedicated time to developing individual writing with two professional writers, include a midweek reading by a third visiting writer, take place in beautiful houses in inspirational settings, run from a Monday to Saturday and are fully residential providing a unique writing opportunity for people of all ages.

Grants available to all

For details of courses, fees and grants for 2003 please see our website:

www.arvonfoundation.org

or contact

The Arvon Foundation
National Administration
42A Buckingham Palace Road
London SW1W 0RE

The Arvon Foundation is a registered charity (Charity No. 306694) and a company limited by guarantee (registered in London No. 1086582)

Arvon is supported by
Arts Council England

New from Egg Box Publishing:

The long-awaited first collection from one of the country's most acclaimed new poets, Ramona Herdman.

'New poetry at its sparkling, thrilling best.'
Julia Bell

'An exciting new poetic voice... a highly auspicious debut.'
Hugo Williams

'Such nerve and verve she keeps you wishing for more.'
Esther Morgan

Come What You Wished For
Ramona Herdman

0-9543920-1-9

The unforgettable debut collection from a striking and disturbing new voice, Richard Evans.

'Slips down with all the ease of an innocent-looking white pill.'
Concrete

'Buy this.'
Martin Newell, of the Independent

'Talented, intelligent and sensitive.'
George Szirtes

0-9543920-0-0

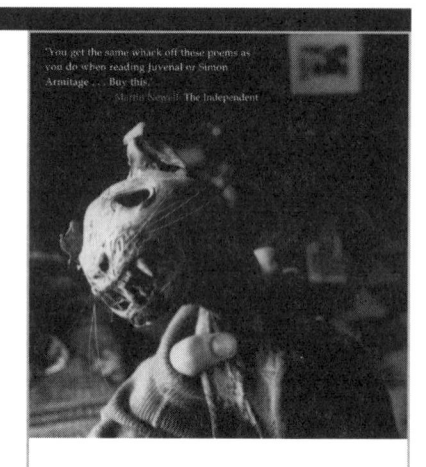

the zoo keeper
richard evans

Out now for £5 each from all good book shops, or from boxofwords.com